DARK PROPHECY

LYNETTE EASON

LYNETTE EASON LLC

Dark Prophecy
by Lynette Eason

ABOUT THE AUTHOR

Lynette Eason is the bestselling author of Oath of Honor, Called to Protect, and Code of Valor, as well as the Women of Justice, Deadly Reunions, Hidden Identity, and Elite Guardians series. She is the winner of three ACFW Carol Awards, the Selah Award, and theInspirational Reader's Choice Award, among others. She is a graduate of the University of South Carolina and has a master's degree in education from Converse College. Eason lives in South Carolina with her husband and two children. Learn more at www.lynetteeason.com.

tomorrow? She tried to remember everything she'd speed-read and thought that rang a bell.

"An hour ago," Riley said, "I got a text from her that simply said, 'Help.'"

"Which led you to rushing into my office screaming like a banshee."

"I didn't scream." Who cared anyway? "And if you'd done your job the first time I asked, we wouldn't be here." They'd promised to check it out. Twelve hours later, after Riley's tenth call, they'd finally said Beth wasn't there.

Riley knew she was.

She'd jumped in her car and made the three-and-a-half-hour trip to the police department of Little Switzerland only to find out the cops hadn't done anything more than simply knock on the gate and ask if Beth was there. When told she wasn't, they'd left.

Which was why Riley now found herself arguing with the scowling sheriff. And getting nowhere. "I *know* they're keeping her here somewhere—against her will—and you're letting them get away with it."

Help.

One word from an unknown number, but Riley had known it was from Beth. She couldn't explain how, she just did. She'd texted back immediately and gotten no response. And now the sheriff was refusing to help—or at least help in the way she thought he should.

Saunders slapped his hat on his head and waved a hand in the air. "You came storming in our office *yelling* that your friend was in some kind of danger from these good folks and refused to leave until we tromped up here to investigate. Again. Well, we did, and guess what? She's not here. We talked to the leaders. Again. We searched the place. Again. Now, we're leaving and so are you." His nostrils flared. "Before I arrest you for trespassing and anything else I can think of."

"But—"

"Don't. Just don't. I'm not playing, little girl. You've disrupted my department—and this compound—two times too many. We're done."

Little girl? Riley saw red and blinked until it faded. She bit her tongue on the lashing she wanted to dish out. Now wasn't the time to fight. Sometimes the wiser option was retreat—or at least the *appearance* of retreat.

She dropped her shoulders and sighed. "Fine. I'll keep calling and texting and hope she answers." She wasn't going to change his mind, and the last thing she needed was to push too hard and wind up in jail for . . . whatever reason Sheriff Saunders decided was plausible.

He raised a brow, then narrowed his eyes as though he didn't quite believe her. "Jennings?" he shouted, keeping his eyes on Riley.

"Yes sir?"

"Come here."

Deputy Jennings trotted over. The good-looking officer gave her a hesitant smile then cleared his throat. "What you need, Sheriff?"

"You searched this compound, right?"

"Yes, of course." He frowned. "Three of us did."

"And you didn't see any sign of the woman?"

Jennings crossed his arms and narrowed his eyes. "Come on, Sheriff, really?"

"Right." The sheriff hitched his belt. "Satisfied?"

"No," Riley said, "not at all, but what else can I do?"

"Exactly. I'm glad you see reason. Go home. Your friend

is probably just hanging out somewhere or holed up working on a story. You'll see."

"And if she's not?"

He sighed. Paused. Then nodded. "If you haven't heard from her in the next twenty-four hours, come back and we'll discuss putting out a BOLO on her. But as far as I'm concerned, she's not here."

He climbed into his cruiser and sped away. Two other deputies followed behind him, leaving Riley to stare at the now shut—and locked—gates while she pondered her next move. Wait twenty-four more hours when she was scary-certain Beth was in trouble?

Absolutely not.

Shortly before she'd gotten the text from Beth, she'd texted Steve Patterson, her former boyfriend—and current headache—to cancel their lunch date. Correction, their noon *meeting*.

She'd given him a brief sketch of the situation and he'd texted back that he was on the way to help. She'd told him she was fine and could handle it, but knowing him, he was on the interstate headed her way.

Steve was a protector. It was in his blood. It didn't mean he thought she was incompetent or helpless, it just meant he was determined to help in whatever capacity he could.

Which might not be a bad thing in spite of their rocky history—and the fact that she was keenly aware that speaking to him—being in his presence would rip the band-aid off the wound that still wasn't healed.

She pulled out her phone and sent a group text to her friends and coworkers to fill them in, and she knew they'd be on the way as soon as they could. Riley also knew she'd probably need their help.

Because there was no way she was leaving this place without her friend.

KATIE MATTHEWS RUSHED into the Elite Guardians office, cell phone clutched in her right hand. Her friend and coworker Olivia Savage sat at her desk typing on her keyboard, brows furrowed, lips twisted in concentration.

"Did you get a text from Riley?" Katie asked.

Olivia's fingers paused, but her glare remained on the screen. "No, why?"

"Check your phone."

"I heard it buzz," Olivia said, her features finally smoothing. She grabbed her phone from under a pile of papers. "I was trying to finish up this report." She read the text and gasped. "What in the world? She's not ready for something like that." She stood and grabbed her keys.

"No kidding. None of us would go in there alone."

Olivia raised a brow. "We would if we thought we had no other option—and that backup was on the way."

"True enough." They headed out the door. "Should we tell Charlie to meet us there, too?" Charlie was the only male on staff with Elite Guardians.

Olivia shook her head, leading the way to her new Chevy Suburban. "He's covering that politician's dinner."

"Lizzie?"

"Same dinner."

Maddy was home with her new baby, and Haley and her husband were out of the country. "Guess it's us then. Steve's almost there, I think."

"Steve?" Olivia raised a brow.

"He and I've been talking." Katie slid into the passenger

seat. She'd known Steve since he was a senior in high school and dating Riley. And she'd been there for Riley to help pick up the pieces when Steve had chosen to drop out of her life six years ago. "He wants to win Riley back."

One eyebrow went up and Olivia shut the driver's door. "Good luck with that."

"I know. They were supposed to have lunch today to talk things through."

"Well, I don't know how I feel about that. I remember how hurt she was when he left. It took her a long time to get past that."

"She never got past it," Katie said, her voice soft. "She moved on, but she never stopped missing him—and wondering how he could leave her like that."

Olivia nodded. "Well, be that as it may, the fact that he's near Riley makes me feel a tad better." She pressed the button and the vehicle purred to life. "Did you text her and tell her we're on the way?"

"Getting ready to." Katie buckled her seat belt then tapped out a text.

Stay put, we're coming.

The only problem was, they were about three and a half hours away. Four, if traffic was bad. Katie placed a hand on her friend's arm. "Head to my house. We'll fly."

"Exactly what I was thinking."

"I'll call Daniel."

2

An hour and fifty minutes after the officers left, Riley studied the exterior of the compound. *I'm coming, Beth. Just hold on.*

Using the machete, Riley punched through the next wall of vines and made her way to the copse of trees just before the gated entrance.

One would think she could have found something a little more high-tech to help make her way through the woods, but no, not in the little store at the base of the mountain. She'd found a machete. Seriously? But she hadn't wanted to take more time to search for something else.

Shortly after Saunders had left the compound, Riley had followed, the plan formulating as she drove. Twenty minutes down the mountain, twenty minutes at the library to print things from her iCloud account and get organized so she wouldn't be going in blind, twenty minutes in the general store, and twenty minutes back to the compound.

Only this time, she was going to have to be creative in entering. Thirty more minutes had passed since she'd made her way back to the compound and found her current spot.

She glanced at her phone. Steve should have been close by now, but nothing from him. She squashed the hurt, telling herself she shouldn't be surprised. Not really. Not after the way he left her six years ago.

They'd been high school, then college sweethearts until he'd darted off to join the Marines at the end of their junior year. He'd left barely acknowledging her presence and had communicated about as well while he'd been gone. The anger simmered, but if she was honest, she was more hurt and confused than anything else.

He'd come home two months ago wanting to pick up where they'd left off—or some version of it. "Not likely," she muttered.

Although she had to admit she wanted to. Which was probably why she'd convinced herself that meeting him for lunch was okay. She'd planned to flat-out ask him what his problem had been, hear him out, and walk away.

But a little niggling in the back of her head taunted her with the question of whether she would have actually followed through with that plan.

She pushed away thoughts of Steve and scanned the compound again. She really didn't want to do this on her own. It would be incredibly risky, but it didn't look like she was going to have much choice. Beth's one-word text kept flashing in her mind. What if she was too late already?

Hovering behind the huge oak trunk, Riley studied the concrete walls with bars on the windows, locked gates, and cameras around the perimeter.

Old-model cameras that would produce grainy black-and-white pictures but still had the power to ruin everything if she wasn't able to get past them. If they had so many high-ranking, high-profile members, why didn't they upgrade their security? Or was it all just for show to make them look less fortified, less prison-like, than they actually were?

Why would anyone choose this over the freedom to come and go as they pleased? Then again, not everyone had it as well as she did. While she'd suffered agonizing grief at the loss of her parents, she'd had her Uncle Daniel step up and give her a loving home. And after he'd married Katie, things had just gotten even better. She was loved. She had a support system. Not everyone had that.

When she thought about it that way, she supposed she could understand the draw of the place. The facility was known to attract people looking for peace, a lack of drama, simpler times, and a community that cared about one another. What was *not* to like? Right?

A whole lot, as far as she was concerned. And after the experience with the cops and the leaders, she was even more skeptical.

Beth would never just disappear like she had. Her friend had done in-depth research, and her notes included a map of the compound and the names of people who'd sold businesses and homes in order to give the money to Ivan and join the minimalist cult. Donors that included Beth's thirty-year-old brother, the whole reason her friend was so interested in—or obsessed with—the cult.

Out of range of the cameras, Riley studied the gates. In addition to Beth's notes, Riley's earth-mapping software had told her a lot about the compound, including one area that looked like she might be able to breach without being seen or setting off any alarms.

Maybe.

As she made her way around the perimeter, using the printed map to avoid the wires that would trip alarms—

again with the old-fashioned security—she thought about the ladies she worked with.

Olivia Savage, Katie Matthews, Maddy Holcombe, and Haley Rothwell had been major influences in her life since her uncle Daniel had become her guardian and then married Katie.

A group of elite bodyguards, they'd taken Riley in and trained her to be one of them while Riley had worked hard to earn her college degree. They'd always been there for her and they'd come through this time. As soon as they got her messages. Which they should have by now.

So why hadn't she gotten a response? Not even from her uncle. Weird. She glanced at the bars at the top of the screen and groaned.

No signal. Really?

She frowned. She'd had a signal at the bottom of the mountain while in the library, but not since she'd been back on the mountain. But she remembered having a signal when she'd been arguing with the sheriff. Double weird.

Maybe it would come back once she was in a different area. Riley once again pondered the idea of going back down the mountain and waiting for the others to arrive, but Beth was in trouble.

Still no word from Steve either. Because he hadn't responded, or because she had no signal to actually receive the response? The truth was, she was glad he was on his way. She'd take his help and be grateful for it if he could get there in time to give it.

And what about the others? She tried to send another text to Olivia.

How far away are you guys?

The blue bar ran across the top of the screen then stopped. She hadn't really expected it to go, but she'd had to try. Riley rubbed her eyes and considered the implications. No cell signal, no real way to know where her backup was. She tucked the phone away.

It was time to make her way in and pray she was right about the vulnerable spot in the fence—and about her friends being on the way.

Because if she was wrong, she was going to be in as much trouble as she suspected Beth was.

STEVE PATTERSON TROMPED through the wooded area, his gaze fixed on the trail left by the woman he wanted to strangle. Okay, maybe not literally, but Riley was about to drive him to the brink of madness. He continued following her path while he shot a text to Katie.

On her trail. She's definitely headed to the Swiss Saints compound like her text said.

At least she'd texted him to break off the lunch date and hadn't just stood him up. He had to admit that gave him hope.

Beth is missing, she'd said in her group message. *She texted 'help' from an unknown number. No response when I answered. I called the cops and they acted like it's nothing. I have to get her out of there. She left a date. July 14th with the letters EOW? My gut says something's happening on that date-tmw. Could EOW = End of the World? I need to find her fast in case this is another Jim Jones, mass-suicide thing going on. I'm heading to the Swiss Saints compound to get her out of there. I might need some backup. I'm sharing my location so you can find me and adding directions to the compound.*

That was three hours ago.

Olivia and Katie were on the way. He'd just gotten a head start on the ladies because he'd bolted after her the minute he'd gotten her text about why she was cancelling their lunch date.

Steve grunted. On the way to the compound, he'd had a friend do research and give him a running commentary on the Swiss Saints.

According to the friend, the group didn't seem that bad. On the surface anyway. But, his friend had said, there was plenty of speculation about what went on behind the walls of the compound.

Like drug and gun running. Human trafficking. Child abuse disguised as marriage. And more. Steve curled his fingers into a fist. With those rumors swirling in his mind, it wasn't likely Riley's arrival would be welcomed.

His friend had also reported that once a person passed through those barbwire-topped gates, they didn't come back out. At least that was the rumor for a number of the disappearances in the area.

And because Riley thought Beth was behind those gates, she planned to enter them—or some part of the fence, knowing her.

"Stubborn," Steve muttered. "Stubborn, pig-headed, crazy . . ." Beautiful, smart, feisty . . .

All of the above.

The many reasons he'd thought about her every day for the past six years that he'd been gone. Steve had known winning Riley back wasn't going to be easy, but he hadn't expected her to completely shut him out, either.

When he'd gone looking for her, he'd found the Elite Guardian's first annual cookout in full swing. Uncertain what to do next, he'd slipped into the hangar to think.

Only Riley had stepped inside seconds later and his heart had slammed into his throat.

And he'd known.

Known without a doubt she was the one for him. Known that he'd been wrong to let his father's words influence him. So very wrong to leave her with no promises. He'd been wrong about a lot of things. The minute Riley had seen him, she'd done an about-face, disappeared back into the main house, and had refused to come back out. No amount of pleading had convinced her otherwise.

So, this was it. He was going to find her and beg her to listen. He just had to keep her out of trouble long enough to tell her all of that and convince her to give him another chance.

He glanced at his phone and noted the text hadn't gone through. He tried again. Then realized it was hopeless because he had no signal.

Great.

～

KATIE STUDIED the laptop as the plane shot through the sky. Olivia had snagged a Coke from the refrigerator and returned to settle in the seat opposite her. "Who is this guy, Applewood?" she asked, buckling her seatbelt. "Who are the Swiss Saints?"

"I've heard of them," Daniel said from the pilot seat, "but only in passing."

Olivia looked at Katie. "Have you found anything?"

"Well, I haven't had much time to research, but it looks like the cult started out in California. The leader of it, a Paul Applewood, was sentenced to life in prison a year and a half ago."

"What for?" Olivia asked. Katie studied the screen, then looked up and met Olivia's eyes.

"What?" the woman asked.

Katie curled her fingers into fists before forcing them to relax. "Murder," she said. "He was charged with murder and found guilty. They found the bodies of five young girls buried on the property, around the perimeter of his 'dwelling place.'"

Olivia frowned. "That's not good."

"He prophesied the end of the world using all kinds mathematical formulas." She scrolled. "When the world continued on, he had some kind of excuse why nothing happened. His believers bought it, but it was soon after that he was arrested and the cult disbanded. The father went to prison, but was almost killed twice before they learned a price was put on his head. They moved him all the way out to North Carolina as a precaution—and it seems to have worked. No more attempts and he's been quietly serving his time like a good little prisoner. It looks like his son, Applewood Junior—Ivan—moved out here. He started the cult back up—and get this, he has a blog and he says the world will end tomorrow."

"What? Seriously?"

"That's what his prophecy is. He just posted that little tidbit this morning." She tapped a few more keys on the keyboard. "Paul also has a daughter named Lila, but no known address is coming up. Looks like she left the cult a couple of years before her father was arrested."

Olivia frowned. "Where'd she go?"

"Doesn't say. I'll see if Annie can track her down." Annie was a technical analyst with the FBI and could find just about anything that needed finding. Katie had worked with her for a few years before deciding she needed a change of occupations. She sent the email, then clicked on the next screen. "There aren't any complaints filed against the current cult and no record of any arrests of any of the members." She paused. More clicking. "Everything looks like it's on the up and up—wait a minute. Back up. I've got something here. It looks like there actually *was* a complaint from one of the neighbors who lives on the mountain near the compound. The complaint was filed in the early morning hours of . . . yesterday."

"Yesterday?"

"Yep." She fiddled with the software until she was able to zoom in. "That neighbor lives just off the main road that leads to the compound. She stated that trucks were coming and going at all hours of the night for the past five nights. She said she'd just gotten a new puppy and had started setting her alarm to take the puppy out for potty breaks. That's when she started noticing the trucks coming and going. By third night, she was convinced something weird was going on and she wanted to know where the trucks came from, so she waited up and followed them to the compound. Once the gates closed, she was done. At least until her report to the police."

"Gutsy. And she's never noticed them before?"

"Apparently not."

"Did the police investigate?"

Katie clicked, looking through the report she'd requested. "Yes. Their findings included nothing suspicious and they told the neighbor there wasn't anything they could do about the noise. The people in the compound had as much right as she did to come and go as they pleased—even in their noisy trucks."

"Well, that's true enough," Olivia said. "But still . . . the neighbor has never complained about anything before. Why the sudden uptick in activity at the compound?"

"No way to know." Katie shrugged. "Could be anything, but I'll admit, I'm suspicious and don't think it's anything good. The compound itself looks harmless. Rows of houses, a larger building that looks like it might be a church. Another, smaller group of houses . . . maybe cabins?" She ran the mouse over the screen. "And something could be a community center or gymnasium on the big hill in the northeast corner."

Olivia nodded. "I've got the layout in my head. Now, we need to find Riley."

"And her phone's still going to voice mail. GPS tracker is off on it, too."

"Fabulous."

3

At the edge of the tree line, Riley stripped off her outer layer of clothes and watched the camera. It was the kind that moved from side to side in a ten second rotation. Ten seconds to the right. Ten seconds back. She'd clocked it four times just to be sure. The only problem was, she didn't know if the camera's range reached all the way up against the fence or if she would be "invisible" just under it.

She *thought* she'd be out of sight. It was a gamble she'd have to take. Quickly, she pulled the other clothes out of her backpack and dressed, continuing to monitor the camera and to determine whether anyone appeared to be guarding this area of the fence. No one did—which was what she'd hoped for—but she didn't blindly trust that it would be so.

According to Beth's notes, everyone inside the compound should be in the dining hall eating together as one big family. Dinner was a community event, and no one missed it short of a catastrophic illness, the birth of a baby, or tragedy.

Riley figured she only had to dodge any guards Beth had noted patrolling the perimeter and inside.

On the next rotation of the cameras, with cutters in hand, Riley darted in and cut the chain-link fence. After tossing the uncomfortable black clogs through the hole, she scrambled through and let the fence parts fall back into place.

She quickly buried the cutters in the dirt and prayed no one noticed the cuts or the disturbed earth. Because that was going to be their way out as well.

Keeping her head down, she smoothed her hands down the black skirt, shoved her feet into the clogs, and tugged at the collar of the short-sleeved white blouse. Satisfied with that part of the cult uniform that had so nicely been on sale at the little general store, she pulled the black hair net from the pocket of the skirt and quickly fixed her French braid. Finally, she donned the purple head scarf exactly like she'd seen in the pictures from Beth's file.

Appearance-wise, Riley should fit in just fine.

"Okay, here goes everything," she whispered. First things first. She needed a place to hide until dinner was over and she could watch the comings and goings of those in charge.

She closed her eyes and pictured the layout she'd memorized. It was small compared to some she was familiar with, but still a good amount of territory to cover. According to Beth's notes, there were about a hundred people living on the property. Hopefully enough that she would blend in.

To the right of her were the single women's dorms. To the left the single men's. Both had laundry on the lines, clipped with clothes pins and blowing in the breeze. So . . . no electricity? Or simply a choice?

She didn't remember Beth's notes saying anything about no power in the compound. And the cameras were rotating, so there was power coming from somewhere. At the top of the horseshoe-shaped area lived the six women who'd married the leader. Together they'd produced twenty-two children ranging in age from newborn to fourteen.

Just behind that was the auditorium that faced the man-made lake, complete with boat dock and floatplane landing area. The plane was missing, but two boats were tied to a post.

Scurrying toward the dining hall, she couldn't help but wonder where the plane was. Beth's aerial photos had shown it docked there. The lake was only about three hundred feet at its longest point. It would take some real skill to take off and land in such a short distance.

But it could be done.

She'd flown a few floatplanes. They weren't her favorite and she had no desire to do it again, but she could admire the pilot who did. The lake itself was surrounded by a wrought iron fence with concrete walls in the process of going up.

Riley knew she'd lucked out. It wouldn't be long before they finished the wall and the entire compound would be enclosed, making it much more difficult to get in—or out.

She found the dining hall easily enough and stepped to the side of the building to watch the door. Soon, a throng of women in black skirts, white shirts, and purple head coverings emerged from the wooden structure.

Riley waited until a group passed her then merged with them, keeping her head down. She fell into step behind the last straggler, thankful they were walking slowly and talking quietly amongst themselves.

Children dressed in miniature versions of the uniform ran and played, laughing, happy, still innocent and unaware that the world their parents had brought them into wasn't normal—or safe.

Riley's throat clogged. Somehow, she'd find a way to get them out. As soon as she found Beth.

"Who are you?"

The voice froze her and she looked up to find a woman about her age standing in front of her, a squirming infant on her hip, brows drawn over dark green eyes.

"I'm Riley," she blurted. "I just got here today."

"But you're always supposed to stay with your guide so you don't get lost or overwhelmed."

Guide? Oh yes, the guide from Beth's notes. Rats. "I . . . I know. It's not her fault. I got curious and kind of wandered off."

"But weren't you told the consequences of that?"

Oh boy. Riley cleared her throat. "I, ah, probably was, but to be honest, I don't think I processed everything I was told."

The frown disappeared from the woman's face, but a flash of anxiety centered itself in her eyes. "I can understand that. That's why you have a guide to help you. Who's yours?"

"My guide? Um . . ." Riley forced her eyes to tear and twisted her hands, drawing on all of her amateur acting skills. "Oh no," she whispered. "I've forgotten her name. Sarah? No, Simone? Or was it Jasmine?"

"Selah?"

"Yes! Selah. That sounds right. I think." She bit her lip then let it quiver. "I really don't want to get in trouble. Or have Selah get in trouble because she lost me. We stopped at one of the restrooms and she went inside and I . . . well . . . I . . ." Riley held her hands up, trying to look as innocent as possible.

"You *wandered off*."

"Yes, but I didn't mean to go quite so far, and I think I'm lost. Can you point out her home and I'll hurry to it?"

"Her dwelling place."

"Right. Her dwelling place." Not home. Dwelling place. "I'm still learning, sorry."

"It's okay." Compassion and kindness eased the anxiety from the woman's face.

From the corner of her eye, Riley caught movement near the row of smaller structures just beyond the dining hall at the edge of the property. Ten in all. A woman with a tray stood at the door of the second one in the row and knocked. "Is someone sick?" Riley asked.

The woman shifted the toddler to her other hip. "No, that's Repentant Row. Didn't Selah tell you?"

Repentant Row? "We didn't get that far. What's it for?"

The young mother smiled and her wiggly child finally settled, leaned his head against her shoulder, yawned, and stuck a thumb in his mouth. "To repent and become clean again after perpetrating a wrong on the community."

"What do they do to you there? How do they make you repent?"

The smile flipped into a frown. "Whatever it takes to ensure you are clean again. There is a lot of praying and asking for forgiveness, of course."

"Of course."

"I'm not sure about anything else. I've never had to go there."

Riley's stomach turned. "Oh goodness. Will *I*? Have to go there? I meant no wrong." But she was willing to bet that she would find Beth in one of those Repentant Row structures—and her first stop would be the one that looked like it had activity.

"I don't think so. Not if you find Selah. She lives with her

sister and three children on the west end of the compound."
She hefted the child who'd fallen asleep. "I'm Tracy and this
is Cole. It's good that you've come when you have."

"What do you mean?"

"Why, haven't you heard? The end is near. Being here,
you're one of the chosen ones."

EOW? "The end of the world? You believe it's really
ending?"

Tracy simply smiled. "Follow me and I'll show you to
Selah's dwelling place."

"Wait a minute. I want to know about the end of the
world. How does he know?"

"He's the wise one. He receives the word and the word is
always with him."

Riley's stomach lurched. But anger boiled at the decep-
tion perpetrated by a liar.

"Follow me." Tracy started toward Selah's dwelling place
and Riley hurried to catch up.

"Don't you need to be somewhere?" *Think, Riley, think.*
How could she get rid of the woman?

"Soon. I'll need to help get the children ready for bed,
but I can walk you over there."

"No." Riley placed a hand on the woman's arm and she
stopped walking. "Really. I don't want to inconvenience you.
Cole looks like he's getting pretty heavy. Just point it out to
me and I'll find her."

For a moment Tracy hesitated, then she shrugged. "My
dwelling place is halfway there. I'll walk with you and then
I'll point out where to find Selah."

"Great. Thanks." Once the woman was safely inside her
home—she mentally refused to call it a *dwelling place*—
Riley would find a spot to hide, then wait for dark before
she made her way over to Repentant Row.

STEVE LOWERED the binoculars and frowned. He'd been too far away to stop Riley from slipping inside the compound but figured he could do the same once the sun went down. The problem was, he was cut off from all communication with the outside world now. If they ran into trouble, they'd be on their own—at least until Katie and Olivia figured out how to reach them.

A glance at his watch said he had a couple of hours, so he settled next to Riley's original hiding place and prepared to pass the time by keeping watch on the compound, praying he'd get a glimpse of Riley every so often to reassure himself that she was safe—or at least still alive.

He could run down the mountain, make a call for help, and get back to his hiding place all in about forty minutes. But he wasn't comfortable doing that. Riley was in there, and if he left and something went wrong, he'd never know it, much less be able to find a way to help.

Frustration warred with worry for Riley. She'd gone off like Katniss Everdeen, thinking she could handle this alone. And while she was a fighter with some serious skills, she wasn't a warrior.

Okay, so she'd made sure someone knew where she was and she was correct in assuming they'd drop everything to come help, but he was still perturbed with her. Scared for her. He wanted to protect her from the dangers of the world even though she was a very capable woman.

A memory flickered. They'd been checking out at the grocery store and a young mother had run to the front screaming that she couldn't find her child. Riley had jumped in and demanded the store go on lockdown, then hurried the manager to view the security footage.

The child had been found hiding in one of the closed cashier stations, angry that she couldn't have the bag of cookies she wanted. All had ended well due in part to Riley's quick thinking and willingness to act.

Once they were back at her home, her adrenaline had crashed and he'd held her for a long time watching her sleep and running his fingers through her soft hair.

Steve rubbed a hand across his eyes and said a short prayer. The only thing that gave him a smidgeon of comfort now was the fact that she'd had extensive training in self-defense.

Not that training would do much good against a bullet.

Focus.

He swept the compound once more, the binoculars not picking up much of anything except a few people milling outside their homes. Two ladies chatted as they pulled in their laundry.

Which gave him an idea.

4

Riley shifted in the cramped area behind the Dumpster and pulled the scarf part of the head covering up around her nose. At least it was good for something. While the stench still found its way through the cloth, diluted was better than full strength.

From her position, she could see the building on the hill. The one that was apparently off-limits to all but a few residents. She'd seen two men slip in the side door, a light come on, then . . . nothing.

Riley turned her attention back to Repentant Row and saw nothing to make her think anyone was in one of the cottages—no lights, no curtains fluttering inside the barred windows, nothing.

But the woman with the tray had been there for a reason.

A low hum reached her, and her pulse fluttered at the familiar sound. She pulled the binoculars from her bag and focused in on the plane coming in. Within seconds, she could identify it as a Viking seaplane. A Twin Otter, if she wasn't mistaken.

Okay, interesting. They'd drop six million plus on a seventeen-passenger plane, but their security was almost archaic. It struck her as odd, but for now, she simply filed the fact away as the plane dropped lower and lower until it landed smoothly on the lake and glided toward the dock.

Lights popped on and Riley blinked at the sudden brightness. The plane taxied and pulled under the lights. Riley couldn't help admiring the effortless landing and the pilot who'd made it. Impressive.

The door opened and the pilot climbed out, followed by an older man in khakis and a short-sleeved shirt. He carried a large bag over his shoulder and Riley watched, intrigued as the two men climbed into a waiting truck. Using the binoculars, she followed their progress to the top of the hill where the mysterious building sat, the interior lights giving off a soft glow.

Minutes ticked past and darkness eventually blanketed the compound, but she still waited, the full moon giving off enough light for her to watch the comings and goings of the residents.

Finally, the compound seemed to be settled in for the night. Riley stood, her cramped muscles protesting. She winced and waited for the pins-and-needles sensation to pass before glancing around the side of the Dumpster once more. All clear.

With hurried footsteps, she made her way to Repentant Row, keeping a look over her shoulder, feeling like she'd be discovered at any moment. At the third cottage, where she'd seen the woman with the tray, Riley grabbed the knob and twisted.

Locked.

With a deadbolt on the outside for good measure. She flipped it off and tried the knob again.

Still locked.

Riley slipped around the corner to the window and raised up on her tiptoes to peer in. A small light on an end table gave off a faint glow, allowing Riley to scan the cabin. And there she was. "Beth," she whispered.

Her friend lay curled in the fetal position on a cot in the right-hand corner of the building. The door to her left stood open and Riley caught a glimpse of a toilet. A small table under the window next to the cot held an old-fashioned typewriter and paper. Two wooden chairs were pushed under the table.

A tray with food and a half-finished bottle of water lay on the wood floor near the foot of the bed. If Beth had eaten anything, Riley couldn't tell. She tapped on the window.

No response.

Almost in shock that she'd found her so easily, Riley knocked again.

Still, Beth didn't move.

Was she ill? Drugged? Probably the latter. But why?

All questions that would have to be answered later. She needed to get inside. Riley stepped back and examined the door once more. Kinda flimsy. Could she kick it down? Assuming she could, would she have time to get Beth out before someone came running at all the noise?

Only one way to find out. She lifted her foot—

...and heard a step behind her.

She turned and something stung the side of her neck.

STEVE HAD CRAWLED through the gap in the fence about ten minutes ago. Stealing Riley's brilliant idea of making every effort to blend in, he'd stopped at the clothesline and grabbed a pair of white breeches and a loose-fitting linen shirt. He'd darted back to the tree line near the fence and changed clothes, deciding he looked like he was ready to set sail on a pirate ship from the 1600s.

All that aside, he had no idea which way to go once he was inside the compound. He was going to have to go house to house and building to building and see if he could spot Riley before someone caught on to the fact that she—and he—didn't belong.

Only the fact that no alarms had sounded kept his worry from shooting off the charts. Where was she? How had she managed to blend in? The place was spread out but not huge, and everyone probably knew everyone else. Maybe.

He checked his phone. Still no signal. Should have brought a satellite phone. But he was wondering if the signal was jammed by something in the compound, not just the result of bad cell service on top of a mountain.

Steve made it to the row of homes he'd snatched the clothing from and paused at the side of the one on the end. He took a moment to get his bearings. The fence lay behind him, just beyond the tree line. Which was smart, he decided. It made the place feel less like a prison.

Deceptive.

Possibly just like the leader of the Swiss Saints and all of his cohorts.

Riley obviously believed something hinky was going on within the fence. The truth was, Steve wasn't so much concerned about that as he was Riley's whereabouts. After he made sure she was safe, they could work on figuring out what the cult was a cover for.

If it was a cover for anything. Riley clearly believed Beth had disappeared for a reason and was now in danger. She was so convinced that she'd gone off on her own and put her own life at risk.

And at this point, Steve thought Riley was probably right. So now to figure out how to find her and Beth and get them away from the compound before anyone realized they were there.

5

R iley groaned and pressed a hand to her head. Where was the truck that had hit her? With effort, she sat up. Swallowed once. Twice. Then raced for the bathroom where she lost the contents of her stomach.

When she was finished, she slumped to the floor and leaned against the wall until the room stopped spinning. Rubbing her eyes, she stood and tried to ignore the weakness invading her, only to throw out a hand and press against the wall. She needed the swaying to stop and prayed she wouldn't pass out.

For a moment, she simply stood there, taking deep breaths and waiting, getting her balance. Slowly, her head calmed. She turned to the sink to rinse her mouth and splashed her face until the rest of the sickness faded and fear reared its head. She stumbled to the window.

Darkness. Of course. But the lights on the hill in the distance caught her attention, and she desperately wanted to know what they were doing in that building. Who was the well-dressed man from the plane?

She unlocked the window and shoved it up. Of course, the bars prevented her from climbing out, but at least she had a bit of a breeze filtering in to relieve the stifling heat in the small cabin.

Footsteps outside sent her scuttling to the side without taking her eyes from the window. A man passed by, paused and looked her way, then walked on.

A guard. Either he hadn't noticed the open window or he didn't care.

Again, the question presented itself. What did this place —a place promoting peace and inner healing—need with a guard? At least one that patrolled at night. She could under-stand possibly needing one at the entrance to the compound to stop curiosity seekers, but why on the inside and at night?

A rumbling engine broke through the silence and she strained to see in the moonlight. The sound came from the building on the hill. A second engine roared to life, then a third. Headlights popped on and began the trek down the steep grade.

Riley let out a low breath and walked to the door. She tried it without much hope, as she figured it was constructed exactly like Beth's had been.

Yep. Locked.

A sliver of moonlight filtered through the window and cut a thin line across the floor, casting shadows on the walls. No small lights for her like Beth had.

In spite of the shadows, she could make out that the hinges were on the inside, and hope flared for a brief second. Until she looked around and realized the bed, chairs, and table were made of wood.

A closer examination confirmed her fear that there wasn't one piece of metal used in the construction of the furniture. It was excellent craftsmanship, but it wasn't going to be any help for her escape.

The bathroom toilet. She could use the top of the tank as a weapon, knock out anyone who came through the door and make a dash for . . . where?

Riley breathed deep. In. Out. In. Out. She refused to allow panic to overwhelm her. She could do this. Surely, someone had gotten her messages and was on the way. Although the compound was easy to find once one reached the top of the mountain, finding the exact road to get there would be tough.

Unless one had specific directions like the ones Beth had left. She'd sent the directions to Steve and the ladies. But had they gone through? Steve's had, but she wasn't sure about the texts to the others. She consoled herself that Steve was out there somewhere, looking for her.

He'd always had her back. When the bullies at school had nearly driven her crazy, he'd stepped in and put them in their place. He'd been there when she'd had a killer after her. He'd encouraged her when she'd decided to fly for a living. He'd always been there.

Until he wasn't.

Which was why his sudden, silent departure been so shattering and confusing. When he'd shown up at the cook-out, she hadn't been able to look at him, much less talk to him. It had taken her weeks to feel stable enough to agree to meet him.

She sank onto the bed and closed her eyes.

A trilling sound floated through the window and she blinked, realized she'd dozed off, and stood. No more sleeping. She had to get out.

Again, the same sound reached her. This time she paused. Frowned. She knew that sound. Almost like a bird calling to its mate in the early morning hours. Only more intense. And shrill.

It came once more, the notes rising and falling. No. Not a bird. Steve! It couldn't be. It had been years since he'd stood outside her window and whistled the tune of the mockingjay from their favorite movie. He'd practiced until he nailed it, then come to find her to show off his new skill. Riley waited, breath lodged in her throat.

Seconds ticked past.

Yet again, the whistle came. Much closer this time. She bolted to the window. "Steve!" She whisper-yelled his name, straining to see. Riley pursed her lips and tried to whistle back, but, just like when she'd tried to learn years ago, she only managed to blow air. She gave up. "Steve!"

STEVE FROZE at the sound of the low whisper drifting to him from the end cottage. He'd already dodged one armed guard and now it looked like he'd found Riley, only to have her alert the second guard, who'd pulled an earpiece from his ear to listen. Steve could only pray she didn't call out again.

He stood on the small porch of the cottage, back to the wall, his fingers wrapped around the Taser he preferred over his Glock.

The guard hesitated a few more seconds, then reinserted the earpiece. He lifted his radio, spoke a few words, then continued his trek down the line of cottages.

Steve let out a slow breath then hurried around the corner to the window. He found Riley peering out. "Hey," he whispered. "Are you ready to get out of here?"

"How did you know where I was?" The relief in her voice made him glad he'd followed his instincts.

"The text helped."

"Yeah. What about Olivia and Katie and the others?"

"They're on the way, but I'm not sure how far out they are. I don't have a signal."

"Join the club."

"I'm coming through the door." He waved a hand. "Don't bean me with that."

"Right." She set the toilet lid down.

Steve checked for the patrolling guards once more, then slipped around to the porch and flipped the deadbolt. He leaned on the knob hard enough and it broke off. He pushed the other section through and heard the thud when it hit the floor. He shoved the door open and Riley hurried to him. "Come on. We have to get Beth. They know I'm here so they may be extra watchful."

"You're very welcome."

She paused and hugged him. "Sorry. I'm very grateful you showed up. Perfect timing."

"That's debatable," he muttered. "How many guards have you noticed?"

"One."

"I've seen two."

"After dinner, everyone went straight to their homes— excuse me, *dwelling places*—and the compound has been a ghost town ever since. Except for the plane landing with two guys who got out, counting the pilot, and whatever is going on up the hill. I saw three trucks come down and leave. At least, I think they left. They were headed for the front gate."

"Well, whatever it is," Steve said, "hopefully, it will keep them distracted long enough to get you and Beth out of here."

"Then let's go."

Steve turned and cracked the door. He looked left, then right then pushed the door open and stepped outside.

Two footsteps to his left. He started to spin only to feel something hard press against the side of his skull. Steve froze, fingers gripping the Taser he couldn't use yet. "Hands over your head and back inside, interloper," the bass voice said in his left ear, "or I'll have no choice but to shoot you where you stand."

Heart pounding, Steve raised his hands.

"Drop whatever that is."

Steve let go of the Taser and it bounced under the bench against the wall. He backed slowly into the room. The man swiveled around so that he was in front of Steve. The gun never wavered and Steve prayed Riley had found a place to hide when she'd heard the confrontation. Only there wasn't a place other than the bathroom—which could be considered hiding in plain sight.

Not helpful.

Once they were both fully inside the cabin, his captor, keeping the gun on Steve's head, reached behind him for the door.

As the door shut, Steve caught sight of Riley from the corner of his eye, her back against the wall, toilet tank lid clutched in both hands. She blinked and looked at the floor. Back at him, then the floor. Without looking at her, he gave a slow dip of his head, not wanting the man behind him to pull the trigger. He took one step back, then two. "What do you want?"

"To remind you reporters to keep your nose out of business that isn't yours."

"I'm not a reporter."

"Then—"

Steve let his legs give out and hit the floor. Riley pounced and swung the toilet tank lid to connect with their captor's head. The man dropped like a rock and the gun thudded to the hardwoods beside him. Steve grabbed it and checked it. A bullet was in the chamber. His stomach churned, but he had no time to dwell on it. "Nice job."

"He's not dead, is he?"

Steve checked. "No. He's got a strong pulse. The headache he's going to wake up with is going to be stronger, but frankly, I don't care."

"Me either." She grabbed his hand. "Let's go find Beth and get out of here."

_____

6

"She's in the cabin next door," Riley said, aiming them toward the door. Once on the porch, Steve shoved the guard's weapon into the waistband of his borrowed pants and grabbed the Taser from under the bench. He wouldn't hesitate to use the gun if necessary but would prefer not to if he could simply incapacitate anyone who got in the way.

With one guard down, Steve kept an eye out for the second one. He stepped off the porch and led the way to the cabin Riley had designated as Beth's prison. "Watch out behind us," he said.

"I'm watching."

He twisted the lock that was twin to the one on Riley's cabin then tried the knob. "It's locked, right?" she asked.

"Yeah."

He set his rucksack on the ground and pulled out a small screwdriver. "These are interior doors. Kind of a stupid thing to do, but . . ." He could break it just like he'd done with Riley's, but this would be much more quiet—and hopefully, wouldn't bring another guard running.

He pressed on the screwdriver, jiggled it, and pushed the door inward. It squeaked as he ducked inside with Riley on his heels. Steve shut the door and prayed no one on the outside noticed the deadbolt aimed in the unlocked direction.

"Beth," Riley whispered. She hurried to her friend's side while Steve strode to the window and glanced out.

"Is she okay?" he asked over his shoulder.

"I'm not sure. She won't wake up."

He moved to Beth's side. "I've had some medical training. Let me check her real quick while you keep an eye out the window."

Steve placed two fingers on Beth's wrist, then the base of her neck while Riley shot him glances. "Her pulse is strong," he said. "I think she's been drugged."

"Yeah, that's what I figured. Probably the same stuff they got me with."

He pointed to the tray. "I don't know what they gave her or how long she'll be out, but at least she's breathing."

"Well, we can't just leave her here. Can you carry her?"

"Yeah, she probably weighs about as much as my rucksack." He studied her for a brief moment. "Once I pick her up, I'm not going to be able to defend us very well."

Riley snorted. "Leave that to me."

Steve studied her for a quiet second then handed her the weapon he'd taken from the guard. She checked it like the expert she was then slid it into the waistband of her skirt. "I'd give anything for a pair of jeans right now." She headed to the door and opened it slowly, peering outside.

"What's up with these stupid uniforms anyway?" he asked. "I feel like a dork."

"No idea."

They weren't really concerned with the clothing, but the

whispered exchange was comfortable, reminding her of past times. Good times. Her nerves steadied and she took a deep breath. "I cut a hole in the fence at the back of the compound."

"I know."

"You do?"

"How do you think I got in?"

She blinked. "Right. So, we head for that?"

"I'm right behind you."

STEVE LIFTED Beth into his arms and followed Riley out the door and into the sticky heat. Even in the mountains during this time of year, it was humid. A crunch to his left stilled him. Riley jerked to a stop and Steve's mind flipped through various scenarios. They'd found the second guard. The man lifted his weapon and pointed it. "Don't move!"

Steve flinched at the shout, expecting every door in the area to open and other armed residents to come running.

With his right hand he shifted Beth.

"Take her back to the cabin," the guard said. Steve moved his hand slightly while Riley gripped the weapon in her right hand, keeping her body turned and the gun out of the guard's line of sight.

"I don't know what's going on in this place," Steve said, "and I don't really care, but we're getting out of here."

The guard held his weapon steady on them with his right hand while he reached for the radio on his shoulder with his left. Steve pressed this thumb to the Taser switch. The two electric cables shot out, catching the man in his stomach.

The guy jerked then went down, his weapon rolling.

Steve dropped the Taser and placed Beth on the ground next to the steps. Riley grabbed the Taser and Steve snagged the guard's gun, tucking it into the waistband of his pants.

Riley waved a hand toward the back of the building. "I'll clean this up, you get him out of sight."

While Riley took care of gathering the Taser and the two caps that had blown off when it was deployed, Steve kept an eye on the surrounding area. All of the dwelling places had blankets over the windows or closed blinds.

No one was watching as far as he could see, although the building on the hill teemed with activity. Hefting the groaning man under his armpits, Steve pulled him into the cabin. Once inside, Steve yanked the cord from the window blinds and bound the guard's wrists behind his back.

"What are you doing?" The words were slurred on a groan.

"Shutting you up until we can get out of here."

The guard laughed. "Getting out isn't an option. They'll stop you."

Steve grabbed a sheet from the bed, and using his teeth, ripped a pieced off. He stuffed it in the man's mouth. "We'll see about that."

Once he was satisfied the guard wouldn't be able to alert anyone anytime soon, Steve opened the door and slipped out to find the porch empty.

"Riley?" he whisper-yelled her name.

"Psst, here."

Her return whisper from around the side of the cabin spurred him down the steps. When he rounded the corner, he found Beth sitting against the wooden wall, blinking and trying to focus on Riley, who crouched in front of her. Riley looked up at him. "She's coming around."

"Hey Beth."

She shook her head. "Steve? Am I dreaming?"

"Nope, I'm here."

She groaned and pressed a palm to her temple. "Oh man, what did they hit me with?"

"Chloroform probably, but who knows?" Riley said. "Right now, we need to get moving."

Beth gasped. "No. Wait. What day is?"

"Uh . . . Thursday," Steve said.

"The date?"

Riley exchanged a puzzled glance with Steve. "The thirteenth." He glanced at his watch. "Well, actually, it's the fourteenth now. Why?"

"We have to find a phone that works. Or a radio. Or something."

Riley frowned. "What's going on?"

"Before I got caught, I was snooping and came across a folder in the office in that building on the hill. On the front of the folder was the date July fourteenth." She stood and swayed. Riley caught her arm and Steve gripped her shoulder. "I think they're planning to do something. Something that involves a lot of automatic rifles and C-4 explosives."

"That doesn't sound good," Steve said. "Let's get out of here and down the mountain. We'll get the cops and tell them what's going on."

"No!" Beth shuddered and pulled back. "I know there's at least one cop involved. In the same discussion I overheard about the rifles and the C-4, I also heard them talking about 'the cop getting his payout,' but I don't know which one, so going to them isn't an option."

"Well, Katie and Olivia are on the way," Riley said. "They'll be here soon. We can go down the mountain and wait on them for backup."

Tears stood in Beth's eyes. "You don't understand.

They're going to kill people. I don't know who and I don't know where, I just know it's supposed to happen today. Maybe not before dawn, but sometime today. We have to find that out so we know where to send the cops—the good ones."

Steve met Riley's gaze. "First things first. We find a phone and get word to Katie and Olivia so they know exactly where to come and to bring help. Help we can trust."

"A phone would be great," Beth said, "but there's only service during certain times of the day—which is how I managed to get that text out to you. This time of night is not one of those times."

"The trucks left," Riley said. "Surely, they're communicating somehow."

Beth nodded. "There's a radio in the warehouse on the hill. And I think that's where the cell phone jammer is."

Well, that explained the lack of a signal. "All right," Steve said, "the trucks left, right?"

"Yes," Riley said, "I watched them drive down the hill and head for the gates."

"Then it's possible no one's in there—or at least only one person standing guard or something."

"I've never seen anyone standing guard there," Beth said. "They're usually there or they're not."

"Then we can get to the radio," Riley said.

Beth nodded. "Or turn off the cell phone jammer, assuming we can find it."

Riley gripped her friend's arm. "Can you make it?"

"Try stopping me."

7

Riley figured Beth's words were more bravado than reality. The entrance to the hill was at least a quarter of a mile away. Not too far for someone healthy, but for a woman with drugs still running through her, it was clearly going to be an effort. Riley could empathize. Her own legs still felt a bit wobbly, but she was determined to push through. If Beth said the situation was urgent, then it was. Period.

"Are you sure you can make it?" Riley asked.

"I told you, I'll make it."

Steve frowned. "You guys want to hide out somewhere while I check out the building?"

"No," Beth said. "Once they realize we're missing, there'll be a full-on search for us." She trembled. "If they catch me again, I'm dead. They trusted me until they caught me snooping. The atmosphere has changed around here in the last couple of days. That's one reason they drugged me, I think. When I realized there were drugs in the water and the food, I forced myself to throw up, but I guess enough got in to knock me out."

Riley met Steve's gaze and his frown stayed put, but he nodded. "All right, then. Let's go."

With Riley and Steve supporting Beth on each side, they started for the building on the hill, staying in the shadows as much as possible. "I don't understand why no one came running at all the noise we made," Steve said. "Other than the guards, I mean."

A grunt slipped from Beth. "They're trained not to."

"How did you manage to send that text for help?" Riley asked.

"When the woman brought my tray for breakfast, she had her five-year-old son with her. The kid was playing a game on her phone and dropped it. It slid under the bed while she was putting the food on the table. I grabbed it real quick and darted into the bathroom. I only had time to type in your number, the text and hit Send before she came in and snatched it from me. She was really angry, but I also knew she wouldn't tell anyone. She would have been punished for being careless with the phone. Not everyone is allowed to have them." Beth lifted a shoulder in a micro shrug. "There wasn't a lock on the bathroom door. I knew I didn't have a lot of time and I knew you'd know it was from me—especially since I missed our check-ins."

"I knew." Riley focused on putting one foot in front of the other. Steve couldn't deal with two weak-kneed females at the moment. "What's with the old-fashioned typewriter?" Riley asked.

"They figured out who I was and wanted me to write a story about the cult—from their perspective. I agreed so that I could snoop."

"Looking for Garrett?"

Her friend tensed at the mention of her brother but kept walking. "Yes."

"Did you find him?"

"I did." A pause. "Or at least his grave."

Riley sucked in a breath. "Oh, Beth," she whispered.

"I know. I'm trying not to think about it." She kept her voice low, her steps growing stronger as the drug wore off. "One of the residents told me what happened. She said he defied an order from Applewood about punishing a teenager. Applewood shot him. Just . . . pulled out a gun and shot him."

"I'm so sorry." Riley's throat tightened and she cleared it.

"I want him put away, Riles. I don't want him to ever hurt another person."

"Yeah. I'm with you on that."

"We're almost there," Steve said. His head had been on a swivel the whole time. "No other guards in sight and there doesn't appear to be anyone looking for the ones out of commission."

"They'll be looking for them soon enough," Beth said. As they approached the tree-lined concrete driveway at the base of the hill, Beth pulled to a stop. "There's not a lot of security in this building—at least not that I could find—but there must be some, because this is where they found me snooping around. I think they rely on the cameras for the most part."

Steve let go of his grip on Beth and stepped in front of them. "All right, let me go ahead. Riley, you keep an eye on our tail."

"Got it."

Steve kept a hand on his weapon and made his way up the hill, using the trees as cover. Riley followed, keeping her arm around Beth. "You didn't have your credentials on you when they found you, did you?"

"No."

"Then how did they find out who you were?"

Beth fell silent. "I'm not completely sure, but I think it was via facial recognition." Her friend dropped her arm from Riley's waist. "I'm feeling better. I can climb this on my own. It's not that steep, just long."

"Facial recognition?" Riley asked. "But . . . how?"

"They took my picture and one said, 'Send it to him.' It's possible one of the cops on the force has a connection with someone in the FBI or some other agency that has access to the program. I don't know, but it's the only thing that I can think of that fits."

Riley thought about the sheriff who'd chased her off and told her to leave things alone at the compound. He'd said they'd searched it, but . . . obviously not. If Riley had found Beth as easily as she had, the sheriff and his two deputies shouldn't have had any trouble.

"Okay, we won't call the cops for help, we'll call people we trust." The problem was, how far away were they?

STEVE NOTED the women talking softly behind him as they finally reached the top of the hill. The driveway leveled out into a large empty parking lot in front of the metal building. The structure itself was about the size of a fast-food restaurant, but looked like a miniature warehouse.

The gray door, which was illuminated by the outside lights, matched the gray exterior. Black bars on the windows deterred curiosity. Something was definitely going on in there that someone didn't want discovered. And yet there didn't seem to be anyone guarding the perimeter of the place.

Was it possible they simply didn't believe they needed

guards in that area? And yet they had them in the compound near the cottages. Which actually kind of made sense. That's where the prisoners were.

But up here . . .

Steve let Riley and Beth catch up with him, next to the tall tree. "How did you go in before?" he asked Beth.

"I simply walked in the front door."

He nodded. "They've got cameras." But was anyone monitoring them? "Right now, I think we're out of range." He paused. "All right, let's trying going in the back."

Scurrying next to the tree line, they made their way parallel to the building and stopped when the concrete and trees ran out. Steve wasn't able to see what lay beyond the building and the lights, but if memory served correctly, it was a large field with more trees and the fence beyond. He slapped the binoculars to his eyes and ran the lenses over the walls, the gutter, the door. Two cameras on the door. None on the walls. "I've got an idea."

Riley looked up. "What?"

"We need to cross that open area and get up against the wall. Once there, we can work our way around to the door."

"And under the cameras like I did at the perimeter to get inside the fence," Riley said.

"That's where I got the idea." He shot her a quick smile. "They're old cameras and they're sticking way out off the wall. They'll still work great for anyone approaching normally, but I don't think we'll have any trouble slipping under them. Follow me."

Steve didn't wait for an answer. His nerves were already strung tight. Staying next to the wall of the building, in the shadows cast by the lights, they walked single file to the back door. "Stay against the building. If your back isn't touching, you're out too far."

"This feels familiar," Riley muttered.

"And almost too easy," Beth said.

Steve hesitated. She was kind of right. It had been relatively simple to reach the building.

"There's really no one here," Beth whispered. "This is so weird."

"How so?"

"This place is usually busy, not covered up with people, but busy. And now everyone's gone."

"That's because everyone probably left in those three trucks," Riley said. "Which means something's getting ready to happen?"

"Yeah," Steve agreed. "Probably. But what?"

8

Riley stepped closer to Steve. "Can you get it open?"

"Gonna have to if we want to see what's in there." He pulled something from his backpack.

"You have lock-picking tools?"

He shrugged. "Never hurts to be prepared."

"True." She wasn't going to lie. The fact that he knew how to use them impressed her.

With a final look at the camera, he slipped to the door and went to work.

Riley turned to give the compound a sweeping glance. "It's like a ghost town down there."

"I wasn't here long before I got caught," Beth said, "but I learned a lot. The residents aren't allowed out after dark unless summoned by Applewood himself."

Riley grimaced. "Why?"

"I don't know. At least, I'm not sure. I have my thoughts, but no proof. That's what I was looking for when I must have tripped an alarm."

Riley looked past her friend to Steve still hunched over the door. "What's taking so long?" she hissed.

He shot her a frown. "It's not as easy as television makes it look, thank you very much."

Rubbing her hands together, Riley shot another look down the hill. "Those trucks were going somewhere," she said. "No pressure, but they've been gone for a while, which means they could be on the way back."

"No pressure. Right." Steve gave a whispered grunt. "We don't want to move too fast, though. They could have left someone inside." Riley heard the lock give a quick snick, and he let out a slow breath.

Crouched to the side, Steve gave the door a soft push. It swung open without a sound. Riley tensed, waiting for someone or something to sound the alarm. When nothing happened, her pulse skittered into a slower rhythm.

"Clear so far," Steve said, his voice low. "Step inside, but hold still just inside the door. I want to take a look and make sure we're not going to set off the same alarm that Beth did."

"You go right," Riley said. "I'll go left."

He paused, then gave her a short nod. "Fine." She pulled the weapon from her waistband and he looked at Beth. "You stay against the wall just inside while we clear the place, okay?"

She nodded.

Once they were inside, Beth planted herself against the wall as asked. Steve vanished into the dark interior, making his way around the perimeter to the right.

Riley stepped quickly along the edge of the building, listening for any sign that someone else was present. The gun felt good snugged against her palm, calming her nerves and sending a shot of steel through her spine.

She made it to the back, dodging furniture and large

crates filled with something she couldn't see. Steve did the same on the parallel wall. He disappeared behind a large crate then stepped around the corner, and she raised the weapon then lowered it, heart pounding. "Clear?"

"Clear. The place is empty. There's an office behind me. I think that's where we should start."

"This side has a lot of wooden crates. I want to know what's in them."

He hesitated. "I really think we should find a phone first."

"You look for a phone or a radio. I want to take a peek so we can offer more information than just the fact we've been kidnapped."

"That's not enough?"

"You know what I mean."

"All right, fine. You check the crates, and I'll check out the office. Go for it."

Riley hurried to the nearest crate and popped the wooden lid. And gasped. Guns. Lots of semiautomatics. She went to the next crate. More guns. And the next. The following three boxes were empty, but then she found more weapons—and something else that caught her attention. "Steve?"

His head popped out of the office. Beth stood next to the door, frowning. "Yeah?"

"Come take a look at this."

He turned to Beth. "Why don't you see what you can find in there?"

"Sure.

Beth disappeared back into the office while Steve strode over to Riley. "What'd you find?"

She pointed. "You see what I see?"

"Yeah," he said, his voice low. "Guns that *used* to be in the box."

"Right." Foam impressions were all that were left of where the weapons had rested. "Ten to be exact."

"So, where are they?"

"I'm thinking they were on those trucks that left out of the compound."

"That's concerning because I don't have a clue what they plan to do with them."

"I think I can help with that," Beth said from the doorway of the office.

STEVE TURNED. Beth held a notebook in her left hand and a satellite phone in her right. "What is it?"

She handed him the phone. "I can't get it to work."

He strode to the office and stepped inside. Riley and Beth followed him. "There's got to be some kind of jammer in here."

"I looked," Beth said. "But that cabinet's locked and there are no key in any of the drawers I went through. Just those car keys on the wall. And a single key on a ring. It didn't fit the door to the cabinet."

"Looks like the key to the plane." Riley raked a hand through her hair then went to the window to the look out. "So far I don't see any sign that someone knows we're here."

"Good. I just need a couple more minutes." Steve pulled a knife from his belt and jammed the blade between the door and the part on the wall. Using it as a lever, he worked it until the lock popped and the door swung open.

"And there it is."

He flipped the switch.

"Someone's going to notice service is back," Riley said. "We need to be quick."

Steve handed her his cell phone. "See if you can get Olivia. I'm going to go ahead and call the local police. They can't all be corrupt."

"No!" Beth stepped forward. "Please. You don't under-stand. I've done massive amounts of research on this place, the local officers and all involved. While I can't find anything significant on the officers, Applewood's daughter is in town and has been hanging around the sheriff's department."

"The daughter?" Steve asked. "Interesting. I thought she kind of dropped off the radar shortly before her father was arrested."

"Exactly. So, what's she doing here? And what's her connection to the sheriff's office?" Beth shook her head. "Until I know those answers, I'm not willing to trust them."

He hesitated while Riley lifted the phone to her ear. "Olivia! Thank goodness." She rattled off a stream of words and Steve focused back on Beth, who offered him the papers she'd snitched from the office. Riley still had the phone pressed to her ear while nodding and pacing in front of the open crate.

"What are these?" he asked Beth.

"Probably what I was looking for just before they caught me snooping around in here."

He studied them in the dim interior light, the words in the top left corner of the first page stilling him. "That's a prison address." He shuffled the papers. "And these are hospital orders from Montgomery Memorial for a heart procedure."

"I know." Beth rubbed her eyes. "It's all starting to make

sense, I think. I overheard them talking about running drills but was never really clear on what kind of drills."

"Maybe the kind that use automatic weapons?"

"Maybe."

"Sounds to me like you overheard quite a lot."

She shrugged. "Well, that was why I was here. I was trying to learn as much as I could about this place and the people living here."

Riley stepped forward and handed him his phone. "Olivia and Katie are almost here. They had to land at an airport about thirty minutes away, but law enforcement in Asheville met them and are escorting them out here."

"We can't wait on them," he said. "We need to go while we can." He caught Riley up on what Beth had said and shook the papers at her. "The prison is Mountain Top Correctional Institute," he said. He flipped the page. "These are transfer orders, too."

"For who?" Riley asked.

"Paul Applewood."

Beth blinked. "Paul Applewood? That's Ivan's father."

"Apparently the man has a heart condition and they're going to transfer him to the hospital for an operation."

"When?"

"I'm not sure." He glanced at Beth. "You said you overheard them talking about drills. Brainstorm with me concerning what the drills could be, based on your knowledge of what this cult is all about." He flipped the page, scanning the information.

"I'd say they're drills in preparation for the end of the world. Each morning, the residents gather in the center of the compound and Applewood tells them of the revelations that he's received from the evening before." Her voice vibrated with her sorrow. "They hang on his every word, follow him blindly. It's heartbreaking."

"But why would they need rifles for that?" Riley asked.

"I . . . I don't know. I can't think of a reason."

Steve looked up. "You mentioned C-4 explosives. What's it for?"

"I'm not sure. Just that they 'were ready.'" She wiggled air quotes around the last two words.

"Ready for what?"

"That's the million-dollar question."

He pulled another sheet of paper from the stack and found it tri-folded. He opened it. "A map of the compound."

Riley leaned over his shoulder. "Someone did a good job with that. It's very detailed. There's Repentant Row and this building." She pointed to several small black *x*'s. "Wonder what those are."

Steve shook his head. "No idea. There are some *o*'s here, here, and here."

"*X*'s and *o*'s? They must mean something."

"I'm guessing it's not hugs and kisses. The person who made the map would be able to tell us," Riley said.

"Yes, but—"

A footfall outside the door sent his hand to the weapon at the base of his spine. He shot toward the open office door, his intent to close it thwarted by a black boot.

And a gun in his face.

9

Riley stumbled backward, then caught herself on the edge of the desk. "Sheriff Saunders? Are Olivia and Katie with you?" She tried to see past him as another officer stepped into view. "Deputy Jennings? What are you doing here?"

"I believe that's our question," the deputy said, holding his weapon steady.

The sheriff shook his head. "We got a call there were trespassers in the compound. I should have figured you'd be the perpetrator."

"I could've handled this, Sheriff," Jennings said from his position by the door. He still hadn't lowered his gun.

The sheriff frowned but didn't take his eyes from Riley. "Never hurts to have backup."

"I found my friend," Riley said, pointing to Beth. "The one you said wasn't here."

Steve turned, placing his body between her and the weapon. "But she was," she said. "Not only that, but she was drugged and being held against her will in one of those Repentant Row cabins. The ones you said you all searched."

The sheriff's eyes darted from one to the next. "I see."

"She wasn't there when we searched them," Jennings said. "And maybe if you'd stay off other people's property, you wouldn't find yourself in trouble," Jennings said.

"Maybe if you'd listened to a concerned friend," Riley snapped, "I wouldn't have had to go looking for her myself —and wind up in trouble."

Still in the doorway, but to the left of the sheriff, Jennings stepped forward, the scowl on his face encompassing the entire room. Saunders held up a hand. "Y'all stop. We could play the blame game all night and get nowhere. Stand down, Jennings. She's got a point. I mean, she found her friend after you said she wasn't here. I can see why she'd be a little perturbed." His gazed turned to Steve. "And who are you?"

"Steve Patterson. A friend of these ladies."

Riley shifted her weapon to the back of her waistband, noting Jennings hadn't so much as moved his an inch. "Could you put the gun away?"

The sheriff nodded at the man. "Do it."

"I want to know what these three were doing in here," Jennings said, lowering his weapon, but not tucking it into the holster on his right hip.

"Looking for evidence that this cult is just a cover-up for gun running," Beth said, holding another stack of papers in her hand. She waved them at the sheriff. "And probably other stuff, too."

Jennings brows rose and Saunders blinked. "I'm sorry, what?"

Riley tilted her head toward the outside of the office. "Take a look in the crates."

His eyes narrowed. "Jennings, check it out, will you?"

Jennings backed through the door, his gaze darting

between the sheriff, her, and Steve. Finally, he turned and looked into the nearest box. His posture stiffened even more and he returned to stand by his boss. "Guns. Lots of them."

A gasp from Beth turned them all towards her. She held up a map and pointed. "This is a map with the route to the hospital highlighted and Micaville is underlined. Something's going to happen there."

Steve took the map from her. "She's right. And sometime before 6:00 a.m. At least that's what I think that time stamp means." He shoved the paper at the sheriff, who took it with a harsh frown.

"That's two hours from now," Riley said. She paused. Took the transfer papers from the sheriff and pointed. "And then there's this."

"What is it?" Steve asked.

"Wait a minute, wait just a minute. It's coming together for me now. The guns, the explosives. The routes. The hospital orders, prison transfer orders . . . They're going to attack the transfer escort," Riley said softly.

Saunders looked up. "What are you talking about?"

"It's the only thing that makes sense. They're going to try to help Applewood Senior escape."

Saunders scoffed. "What? No way."

Jennings shifted. "Come on, Sheriff. Let's get these jokers back to town and let them sit behind bars for a while. Might curb their penchant for trespassing."

"You think they're going to try and help him escape *before* his procedure?" Steve asked, as though Jennings hadn't said anything. "I'm no doctor, but even I can tell that it looks like he's living on borrowed time. They wouldn't risk it."

"Maybe they feel like it's worth trying rather than waiting for him to die behind bars." Riley raked a hand over her ponytail. "I don't know for sure, but that's what it looks like to me."

"There's a doctor here," Beth said. "I don't know what kind, but he and Ivan have been meeting on a regular basis."

"A Dr. Zimmerman?" Steve asked.

Beth nodded. "How'd you know?"

"His name is on the papers. He's a cardiologist."

STEVE LET his gaze jump between the sheriff and his deputy —and the paper with the name of the cardiologist. Something was off, but he couldn't put his finger on it even while his alarm bells jangled insistently.

"Look him up," Riley said to the sheriff.

"Sorry?"

"You have a phone. Can you look him up and find a picture of him?"

With one eye on her and another on his phone, the sheriff tapped the screen while Jennings shifted from one foot to the other. "Come on, Sheriff. What are you doing?"

"Satisfying my curiosity." He turned the phone around to Riley, whose lips tightened.

"You recognize him," Steve said.

"He got off the plane a few hours ago. When I was hiding behind the Dumpster near Repentant Row, I watched the floatplane land and two men get off. One was the pilot. Dr. Zimmerman was the other."

Jennings scoffed. "The lake is quite a ways from that Dumpster. You're saying you could see someone get off the plane well enough to recognize him in a picture?"

"I was using binoculars. So yeah."

Jennings snapped his lips shut and Riley turned her

attention back to the sheriff. "We have their route. You need to call in someone to stop them."

For a moment, the sheriff simply stood there, his eyes narrowed. Steve gave him a moment to think about it. When the man pulled out his phone again, Steve had to admit relief swept through him. "All right," Saunders said, "you've convinced me. I don't like what the evidence is saying. We'll call in reinforcements. Better safe than sorry."

Jennings scoffed. "Sheriff, are you seriously—"

The sheriff's head snapped up. "What is your problem? You've given me nothing but grief since I walked in your office and overheard you saying you were on your way out here."

Jennings popped his weapon up and aimed it at the sheriff. "My problem is that you always have to micromanage. You should have just left well enough alone."

Riley dove to cover Beth and Steve grabbed the weapon from his waistband. A loud pop echoed through the building and the sheriff went down, his face white, blood streaming from the wound in his shoulder. Jennings turned the weapon to the man's head and Steve fired. His bullet caught the deputy and he cried out and spun, his weapon discharging. The bullet went wild and Steve lowered his head and lunged at Jennings, catching the man in the midsection. They shot backwards, out of the office and into the open area. Jennings's weapon skittered across the concrete floor out of range.

The man was strong but lacked skills Steve had acquired in the military. A fist to the temple stunned Jennings long enough to allow Steve to flip him and yank his wrists behind his back. He snagged the cuffs from the deputy's belt and slapped them on, sparing a quick look at Riley, who shielded Beth with her body and kept her weapon aimed at

Jennings. She nodded. "You've got the medical training, so can you check on the sheriff? I've got this guy covered."

Steve darted to Saunders's side. "Hey, let me take a look at that."

"I'm fine," the sheriff gasped, mouth pinched against the pain. "You three need to get out of here now. There's a well-hidden camera in the corner of the office. That's how they knew you were here."

"And called Jennings to take care of us."

"Exactly. I just happened to walk in the office when the call came in. I overheard him asking some interesting questions and decided to tag along."

"And he wasn't happy about that."

"Not at all. I don't know what his tie to this place is, but right now, it doesn't matter. If anyone else is watching that camera, they're going to come looking."

"We have reinforcements on the way," Riley said, "but no way to communicate with them to see how far out they are." She sighed. "I owe you an apology, sheriff."

"Why's that? You were right all along."

"Yeah, but I thought you were a part of it."

"Apology accepted. Someone hand me my phone so I can call for backup."

Riley pointed to the jammer. "His bullet hit it, forcing the jammer into the 'on' position. There's no service according to this." She waved Steve's phone, then paused. "I think we need to evacuate the residents. There's something else on that map that makes me nervous. Especially with all of the talk about the end of the world."

10

Katie pounded on the door to the sheriff's office while Olivia paced, phone pressed to her ear. Two Asheville police officers waited next to the Chevy Tahoe that had transported them from the small airport. One of the officers was on his radio, no doubt giving his superior an update—and possibly trying to locate the sheriff.

Daniel had gone to the twenty-four-hour medical facility at the end of the block to see if he could find someone who knew where the sheriff was.

Olivia finally stuck the phone back in her pocket and shook her head. "Still no answer from the sheriff or Steve, or Riley."

"Great." Katie glanced at the empty street, the darkness broken only by the lamps spaced about ten yards apart. "I would expect the streets to be empty this time of morning, but it seems like someone would be on duty in the sheriff's office."

"It's a small town," Olivia said. "I guess not much crime happens around here."

"Except kidnappings and gun running."

"Well, yeah."

"What exactly did Riley say when she called you?"

"Just that they were okay for the moment and that they'd found Beth and were trying to get out of the compound. Steve was there with them and they were looking for evidence that the cult is actually a front for gun running and other nefarious crimes. She said she thought the sheriff was in on it and wanted us to bring him with us, but how are we supposed to do that when we can't even find the man?"

"In on it?"

"She wanted to see his expression."

"Y'all looking for the sheriff?" a voice asked from the street.

"Yes." Katie turned to see a young man in his early twenties leaning against one of the lampposts. A lock of dark hair hung in a dirty lump over one eye. "You know where we can find him?"

"Nope."

"Okay. Well, thanks for nothing then." She frowned and turned back to the locked office and scowled. Then spun back to the man. "Hey, what's the easiest and fastest way to get up the mountain to the Swiss Saints compound?"

He flipped the hank of hair from his eye. "You know where the dry cleaner is?"

"No."

He pointed and told her. "Go past that to the first road on the right. Follow that all the way up until you see the gates."

"It's that easy?"

"Yep."

"Thanks." Katie turned back to Olivia, who'd just hung up the phone. Daniel had just returned from the medical facility and stood next to her. "I don't like any of this. Let's head to the compound."

"But Riley was specific in her request to bring the sheriff."

"What if he's already up there?"

"True." Olivia shook her head then slid her gaze back to Katie. "How do you feel about breaking into the sheriff's office?"

"I can do that. What are you going to do?"

"Head to the compound. If there are crooked cops, there might be evidence in there."

Katie nodded. "All right." She looked at her husband. "Will you go with Olivia?"

He hesitated. "You sure you'll be all right here?"

"I'm sure. I think this is the least dangerous place compared to what we're hearing about that compound." She waved a hand toward the two waiting officers. "Go."

RILEY STUDIED the map once more, trying to determine exactly what caused the back of her neck to itch, but nothing stood out to her. "I thought I saw some blueprints of this building," she said. "Where are those?"

Beth pointed to the office. "I'll get them."

She returned and passed the pages to Riley with a frantic look. "They're gathering at the bottom of the hill."

"Who?"

"A whole bunch of the residents. They have lights and what looks like weapons. Rifles maybe."

"I thought all the men were gone."

"Apparently not. And it's also clear they're ignoring their training and coming to investigate. There are about twenty that I can see thanks to the moonlight and their lanterns or flashlights. They must have heard the gunshots and are getting organized to come see what's going on."

"Go," the sheriff said. "I'll stay here and figure something out."

"No." Steve grabbed the man and pulled him to his feet. "Jennings will tell them everything, and Applewood will probably order them to kill you. They think the world is ending tomorrow and will follow his orders blindly, completely oblivious to the fact that he's just using them to further his own agenda."

"To help his father escape the transfer," Riley said.

"It's going to be a bloodbath," the sheriff gasped. "We have to warn them."

"Exactly," Riley said. "So let's go."

Saunders leaned against the desk, gripping the wound in his shoulder. "There's no way to hide. You three can at least make a run for it. I'll just slow you down."

"The plane," Riley said. "If we can make it to the plane, I can fly us out of here."

"Perfect." Steve nodded. "The plane it is, then."

"That's a long hike," Saunders said. "There's no way I'll make it. Help me hide somewhere and come back and get me when you can."

He'd be dead by then. "That's not an option," Steve said. "I'll help you." He looked at Riley. "We'll follow you."

She held her weapon ready and set her jaw. "We've got this."

"I know. Now get us out of here and to the plane."

His total confidence in her sent a wave of determination through her.

"Give me Jennings's gun," Beth said. "I know how to use it."

Riley snagged the weapon and pressed it into her friend's hand. She turned to lead the way out of the office with Beth right behind her. Steve pulled up the rear, helping the sheriff stay on his feet.

Riley's adrenaline flowed while her pulse pounded. She'd been in only one really intense situation before while guarding a client with a stalker, but all had ended well there. This would, too. It had to.

She peered out the nearest window. "They're splitting up. Half to the back, half to the front." Her brain clicked. "Let me see that map again. If Applewood needed a way out of this place, he'd have something set up. Are the doors locked?"

"I'll make sure." Beth passed her the map, then ran for the back door where they'd entered. While Beth checked the doors, Riley examined the map once more. "Okay, we're on the hill. If we go up, it's possible a helicopter could land on the roof, but I'm thinking he'd have tunnels going from here. Underground. It's the only possible way out of here."

"Jennings might know," Steve said.

"But he might not say anything in time for us to use it."

"If we go up, we're trapped," Riley said. She looked at Steve. "Do you remember seeing any ladders or a fire escape when you did your look around the building?"

"No. There's nothing, I'm sure of it."

"Okay, then—"

Beth returned, slightly breathless. "Doors are locked and I've moved some stuff in front of them, so if they manage to get them opened, we'll hear it. But they're on the way up."

"They could have a key," Riley said, her gaze still on the map.

"I'm hoping not," Steve muttered. "Riley? Anything?"

"No. Nothing." She gave a huff of frustration. "That's not right. He wouldn't leave himself no way of escape."

Pounding on the front door made her jerk and the map flew out of her fingers. Beth grabbed it and shoved it back to her. "Come on, Riley. Running out of time."

"I know, I know." She bit her lip while Steve looked over her shoulder.

"Okay," she said. "There's the office, there are three closets or storage areas. I recommend checking those."

"We'll go together," Steve said. "It's not going to take them long to breach the door."

"You two stay here," Beth said. "Riley and I can check them fast. The sheriff doesn't need to be moving."

Steve nodded. "Go."

Beth went left, Riley went right. She found the storage closet next to the stairs that led up to the second floor and pulled the door open. Cleaning supplies, a ladder, rags, shelves with paint, and another whole shelf loaded with ammunition. She tapped the walls, the floor, pulled the ladder over and checked the ceiling.

Nothing.

More pounding on the back door. But no one entered.

Beth returned and Riley met her gaze. "Nothing?"

"No."

"They're out there, but I don't think they have a key or they'd already be in here."

She turned and pressed her fingers to her eyes. When she opened them, they landed on the steps. And a hinge.

The pounding intensified and a dull thud shuddered through the building. "They're trying to break the door down," Beth said.

"I hear them. Get Steve and the sheriff. I think I've found our way out." The building rattled again. "And hurry."

Beth rushed off and Riley lifted the area attached to the hinge. A light popped on. Stairs led down. Footsteps sounded behind her and she turned. Steve held the sheriff against him, practically carrying the man. "I've packed his wound with stuff I found in the bathroom, but he's lost a lot of blood."

"I'm still conscious," Saunders whispered, "but not sure for how long."

"Hang in there," Riley said. She nodded to Steve. "You good?"

"Of course."

Of course.

Steve and the sheriff headed down the steps and Riley motioned for Beth to follow. Then she stepped into the area and pulled on the handle to settle the steps back into place. A loud crash at the front door told her they'd moved just in time.

But what if those breaching the building knew about the passageway?

11

"Come on, come on," Katie muttered. "Answer the phone, Olivia." She clicked on the blueprint of the compound, examining every spare inch. "I've figured this out and you need to know the information. Now pick up."

She was talking to herself, but it helped.

The unanswered ring on the other end of her phone didn't.

She tried Daniel's number.

"Katie?"

"Oh, thank God. You need to get away from the compound, now."

"What's going . . . ?"

He faded. "Daniel!"

"I'm back. We found the border where the signal drops out. What is it??"

"The compound is loaded with explosives. Ned Jennings is one dirty cop. His email is full of all kinds of communications with Applewood and Applewood's daughter. They planned this together. She promised to elope with him once her father was out of prison and stashed safely away where no one could find him."

"Great. The daughter who dropped off the radar?"

"That one. They're going to blow the thing up at some point. Like today. Ivan Applewood's been preaching that the end of the world is coming. Well, it's an ending he's creating."

"Oh no."

"Oh yes. Daniel, please . . ." Her voice hitched. "You can't go in there."

He paused and she heard him filling Olivia in on the situation. "Katie?"

"Yes?" She closed her eyes, knowing what was coming.

"We have to."

She nodded. Swallowed. "I know." But she wished she didn't. She'd lived through one too many bomb scares. That's what she'd trained to do. But Daniel . . .

"We have to find them," he said.

"I've already called law enforcement and the bomb squad."

"Good job. We need to go now. I love you."

"I love you, too." She paused. "And Daniel?"

"Yes?"

"Please don't die."

"I'm not planning on it. I'll call you as soon as we have everyone safe. I love you."

He hung up. The door opened and Katie jumped away from the computer she'd broken into with Annie's help.

A dark-headed officer stood there, scowling. "Who are you?"

"Someone who needs a ride." She hurried toward him and gripped his arm. "Come on, you're driving."

STEVE TIGHTENED his hold on the sheriff's belt and pulled the man alongside him through the tunnel. Stockpiled supplies of canned goods, water, paper products, and more crowded the massive shelves lining the walls. "Someone could live down here for a very long time," he said with a low grunt. The sheriff wasn't exactly a small man and he was leaning harder and harder on Steve with each step.

"Where do you think this comes out?" Beth asked.

Steve glanced back as Riley swept her light behind them. "It's hard to tell," she said, "but I'm guessing near the cafeteria area."

"Anyone behind us?"

"Not that I can tell."

"Okay," Steve said, "if this opens into the cafeteria, then in order to get to the plane, we'll have to cross a lot of open space. That might not go well."

"That doesn't make much sense," Riley said softly. "Why would he have a tunnel from the hill to the cafeteria? Why wouldn't he have it come out somewhere that would allow him access to a way out of the compound?"

"Who knows what that guy was thinking when he built this place?" Steve muttered. "Let's just find the end."

A clatter behind them spurred them faster. "They found the opening," Beth said. Her friend tripped and almost went down in her haste to move more quickly.

Riley caught her. "Go easy. We don't need anyone else getting hurt." She paused even as she hastened her steps. "Okay, we need to be prepared. If they found this tunnel, they may figure out where it ends and send someone there to wait for us to come out." Her fingers tightened around the grip of her weapon.

"I'm ready," Beth said softly.

"Steve? How's the sheriff?"

"I think he's passed out. Or close to it." Steve sounded slightly winded, but Riley wasn't worried. He'd make it.

Steve stopped abruptly and Beth ran smack into his back. Riley almost hit her friend. "What's going on? You okay?"

"It forks," Steve said. "We've got three choices. Straight ahead, to the right or to the left."

Noises from behind them reached her and she blew out a low breath. "Wonderful. Okay, pick one."

"I don't know. Beth? You've been here longer. What do you think?"

"I've lost all sense of direction, I'm sorry."

"To the right," Riley said. "I think that way may lead us to the dock which is close to the plane. I'm not sure, but it's the best educated guess I've got."

Without hesitation, Steve hefted the unconscious sheriff over his right shoulder and darted into the tunnel. Beth followed while Riley stayed back, watching. Shadows danced on the walls. They were getting closer.

She spun on her heel and took off after the others, praying she was right. Because if she was wrong . . .

Not wanting to think about that, she focused on putting one foot in front of the other. The shelves continued down this tunnel, filled with enough medical supplies to outfit a hospital. "They were prepared for just about anything. Where do you think they got all of this?"

"From their cardiologist friend, maybe?" Beth said.

A gust of wind blew Riley's ponytail and she inhaled the tantalizing scent of fresh air. "We're getting close," she whispered.

"I feel it, too," Steve said, his voice low. "Faster, y'all. We're almost there."

Riley picked up her pace, glancing back over her shoulder. "I don't think they're behind us, but don't slow down."

"Not to worry," Steve said. He rounded a slight curve ahead only to stop ten steps later. Steps led up. The clouds filtered enough moonlight to enable Riley to know they led to the outside.

She slipped around Steve. "Please tell me he's still breathing," she whispered.

Steve nodded. "But he needs medical care ASAP."

"I'm going up." She placed a foot on the first step.

He stopped her with a hand on her shoulder. "Let me."

"You're the one with medical training. I've got this."

"But—"

She held his gaze without blinking. "We're wasting time."

Steve backed off, hands held in the position of surrender. He pulled his weapon from his waistband and held it ready, aimed at the grate. "If I so much as think someone's out there to hurt you, I'm shooting."

"I'm okay with that." Slowly, with her own weapon held steady and pointed upward, she placed one foot after the next until she reached the top. Taking precious moments, she scanned the area and saw nothing but sky.

And a door in the wall next to her. Clever. The grate would allow ventilation into the tunnels but wouldn't cause anyone to suspect there was a whole tunnel system below the compound.

She twisted the knob and pushed. The door swung inward and she rounded the edge into an open room. An empty open room with another door on the opposite wall.

Riley turned and motioned for Steve and Beth to join

her. Steve picked up the sheriff once again and hefted the man into a fireman's carry. He was tiring, but pressing on. Beth brought up the rear. Once in the room, Steve nodded to the door. "Where does that go?"

"Getting ready to find out," Riley said. She walked over to it and stood to the side before glancing at Beth. "Ready?"

Beth nodded.

Riley cracked the door, peered out, and gaped.

Just beyond was the dock and the plane.

WHEN RILEY STEPPED BACK, Steve pushed close to the door with the sheriff on his shoulder. His muscles strained and he'd give anything to sit down and rest. Soon. As soon as they were on the plane, in the sky, and on the way to the nearest hospital—or body of water where Riley could land and an ambulance could meet them.

He turned back to her and Beth. "Please tell me one of you brought the key."

Riley waved it at him. "Got it off the wall in the office."

Thank goodness. He took another look outside, the weight of the sheriff growing heavier by the moment.

"All right, we're going to have to cross open space." He cut his gaze to Riley. "Did you see what I did?"

"The guards?"

"Yep."

"I saw. So, how do you propose we get to the plane?"

He started to answer when the shots rang out. Steve glanced out to see the guards spin toward the sound and race in the direction of the gate. "I think help is here and I know how we're getting to the plane."

"Who's shooting?"

"No idea, but we can thank them later. Let's go!"

He pushed through the door and took off for the plane, muscles screaming, fatigue dragging him. Riley raced ahead, then Beth passed him.

Riley's feet hit the dock with a thud. She opened the plane door and shot inside. Beth followed and turned, ready to help him maneuver the sheriff inside.

Another shot rang out and pinged off the metal. Shouts followed. Steve settled Saunders into the nearest seat and slammed the plane's door. "Get this thing in the air."

While Riley cranked the engine and did what she needed, he turned to the sheriff to check the man's wound. It had stopped bleeding and the makeshift bandage he'd created from paper towels and duct tape had held well in spite of all of the jostling he'd suffered. Steve grabbed the first-aid kit from its place on the wall next to the door to the cockpit.

More gunshots and the plane shuddered.

Riley hissed something beneath her breath.

"Problem?" Beth asked, her voice low, tense.

"Not sure yet. Hold on."

The sheriff's eyes opened as the plane lifted. Steve patted his shoulder. "Glad to see you're awake." He rummaged through the kit to find better dressing and tape.

"What's going on?"

"Getting you to a hospital."

"No. Gotta stop them. Fly us to Micaville. You said that's where they were going to attack the transfer." He struggled to straighten and grimaced. "You hear me?"

"I hear you," Riley said, "but we're getting you help. I'm just about to the point where we can use the radio, I think. We'll send law enforcement there and they'll take care of it."

"No, I want to be the one to arrest Applewood." His voice

was weak, but the strength of his determination clear. "He played me for a fool. I thought he was the real deal. I thought the world was truly ending. I'm an idiot . . ." His voice trailed off.

Steve clenched a fist then searched for a bottle of water. He found a cooler full. One thing about extremists—they were prepared. "Sorry, but no one knows when the world will end. No one. Only God knows that."

"Yeah." The sheriff licked his lips and Steve held the bottle so he could drink. When he finished, he let out a low sigh and leaned his head back against the seat. "I guess I have some thinking to do later." He closed his eyes for a moment before opening them once more. "But if I'm headed to eternity, my last act is going to be a good one."

"Getting into heaven isn't based on deeds," Beth said. "You need medical help, Sheriff. Let us get you some."

"Got the radio working," Riley said. The plane shuddered and dipped.

"Riley?" Steve asked.

"Unfortunately, we're leaking fuel. I'm going to have to put it down before we're totally empty."

"Put it down near Micaville," the sheriff grunted. "Please. There's a strip of land you can use as a runway. It's not too far from where you say this attack is going to take place."

Riley turned and met Steve's gaze. "I'm going to have to put it down somewhere. The good news is, this thing has landing gear for a surface other than water. The bad news? I don't know if we can make it to the little strip of land he's talking about."

He nodded. "Radio it in. If law enforcement can meet us, maybe we can get there in time. We've got forty minutes before they're supposed to hit the transfer convoy."

"I'm going to call Olivia and Katie, too." She waved his phone at him. "They've been calling nonstop."

"Do it."

Riley got on the phone and Steve turned back to the sheriff, who'd closed his eyes again. He checked the man's pulse and found it strong and steady beneath his fingers, but he knew the sheriff had to be in terrible pain. He grabbed the first-aid kit, scrounged for the painkillers, and dumped four in his hand. "Take these, Sheriff. Won't be as effective as morphine, but maybe they'll take the edge off."

"Drew." The sheriff took the pills and popped them in his mouth followed by a swig of water.

Steve frowned. "What?"

"My name is Andrew Saunders. Call me Drew."

"All right, Drew, when I changed your bandage, you started bleeding again. That bullet is still in there and doing damage. We must get you to a hospital."

Drew grunted. "She's gotta land this plane practically in the middle of this attack. I'm not leaving until it's done. Understand?"

Exasperated, Steve sat back. "You were in the military, weren't you?"

"Marines."

"I figured. Oorah."

"You know it."

The plane lurched and Steve toppled backwards while Beth gasped. "Hang on, people," Riley said. "Here's the update. Olivia and Daniel are almost to the place where we're landing. Katie hacked into Jennings's work computer and found those *x*'s and *o*'s on the map are where explosives are buried. Law enforcement has taken control of the compound, arrested those who needed it, and removed all others to a safe area. The bomb squad is clearing it as we speak."

The sheriff groaned. "He was going to blow the place up and kill everyone. That was his 'end of the world,' wasn't it?"

"Sure looks that way."

"Unbelievable. The evil," he whispered and covered his eyes with his hand for a moment. "So, the plan was to blow up the compound and everyone in it while the attack on the convoy was taking place."

"Appears like that might have been the idea, yeah. Now, I've got to focus on landing this plane."

"Ivan had a cardiologist all lined up to make sure his father didn't die when they snatched him," Beth said. "And, no doubt, they planned to take him back to the compound. That's what all of the medical stuff in the tunnel was for. I guarantee it."

"I don't know what was down the other tunnels," Steve said, "but I wouldn't be surprised if there were some living quarters. It's really quite brilliant. Bomb the place, then move in below it. No one would ever think of looking for him there."

The plane jerked and sputtered, and Riley cast a quick glance toward the others. "Get ready for what could be a rough landing."

12

Riley eased back on the throttle, lined the plane up with the strip of land, and used the last bit of fuel to bring it to a bumping, rolling stop. With a quick prayer of thanks, she opened the door and lowered the stairs just as a Chevy Tahoe with law enforcement markings pulled up. Riley hurried down the steps followed by Beth.

Olivia jumped out of the passenger seat and Daniel bolted from the back. "Riley! Are you all right?" He rushed at her and grabbed her in a smothering hug.

"Yes," she said, giving him a quick squeeze before pulling away. "I'm fine. But we need an ambulance for Sheriff Saunders. How far away from Micaville are we?"

"About ten minutes, I think," Daniel said.

"Then that's where we need to go," the sheriff said from the open doorway of the plane.

"Sir—" Daniel started.

"Either drive me or I'll walk. But I'm going to be the one to put the cuffs on that man."

"Hop in," Olivia said, climbing back in while Steve

stayed close to the man. "I'd appreciate it if you didn't bleed out on us, though."

"I'll do my best." Drew gripped Steve's shoulder. "Now, help me into that monster vehicle and let's go get this guy."

Beth hurried into the very back while Steve assisted the man into the seat behind the driver. Blue lights appeared, and Olivia's phone buzzed. She grabbed it. Spoke into it. "Hold up, everyone, that's Katie!"

Thirty seconds later, the police cruiser stopped and Katie hopped out. "Riley! Beth!"

"We're okay," Riley said.

Helicopter blades beat the air above them and Katie looked up. "That's the FBI. They've radioed the transfer escort and are going to stop it before they get to the ambush location. It's going to come right through here if I remember the plans correctly."

Gunfire spit from the road just behind them. Engines roared and the trucks from the compound bore down on them. Daniel dove for Katie and took her to the ground. Then yanked her up and aimed her for the Tahoe.

Steve's hand gripped Riley's and pulled her toward the vehicle as well. "Get in! Get in!" Olivia's cry came as more bullets riddled the side of the Tahoe and across the top edge of the windshield. But she made it inside the vehicle, ducking down in the backseat with Steve hovering over and behind her. The one officer in front hunkered low.

The other officer, Daniel, and Katie crouched in the back with Beth. It was crowded, but they'd all made it inside the large Tahoe.

When the bullets ceased, Riley looked up, taking in the marks on the glass and noting the holes. At least it hadn't shattered. Might not be bulletproof, but it was reinforced with something. Heart thudding in her ears, she shifted and Steve moved backwards. "Everyone okay?" he asked.

"I am. I think."

The others voiced their okays, and Riley raised her head in time to see the officer in the police cruiser direct his bullet-riddled car toward the trucks. "Oh boy. He's going to need some backup."

"It's coming," Olivia said from the front passenger floorboard.

More blue lights appeared, racing down the highway. The helicopter kept the spotlight on the cult trucks while agents fired on them from above.

The men from the compound scattered like ants, no longer shooting, but looking for escape from the hail of bullets raining down on them. As soon as the gunfire ceased, state troopers and FBI agents swarmed after them.

"To the treeline!" one called as he led the way.

Riley scrambled from the vehicle and spotted a woman still in the last truck, peering out the back window. Her gaze met Riley's. For a moment, Riley hesitated, wondering who she was before it hit her. "Lila!" The woman's eyes widened, and she threw open the door. Riley started to go after her.

"Riley!"

Steve's shout echoed, but it was the fact that the nearest FBI agent grabbed Lila before she went four steps that brought Riley's forward momentum to a halt.

The agent took the struggling Lila to the ground and cuffed her.

"It wasn't my idea! It was Ned's!" Spittle flew from her mouth.

"Here we go," Steve muttered as he stepped up beside her. "They're going to play the blame game."

"Wouldn't expect them to do anything else," Katie said.

"But that's pretty cold, blaming the guy you're supposed to be in love with."

Almost before Riley could blink, members of the Swiss Saints lay on the ground, their weapons confiscated and hands cuffed behind their backs. She darted forward, looking at each face, searching for the one who'd truly been behind all of this.

Lila's glare from her seat in the back of the FBI sedan didn't faze Riley one bit. She and Jennings had been the masterminds behind the plan and her father had been willing to go along with mass murder. Riley hoped they spent the rest of their days in prison with no chance of parole. She went to the vehicle and yanked the door open.

"Ma'am, stop!" The FBI agent guarding the vehicle slammed it. "Step away."

"I need to talk to her."

"She's in custody. Let me see your credentials."

"I was held hostage because of her and I want to talk to her." His brows rose and Riley grabbed hold of her anger. "Please."

He hesitated, then opened the door.

Riley leaned toward the woman who now refused to look at her. "Where's your father, Lila?"

"Like I would tell you anything." The woman's sneer turned her features ugly and Riley clenched a fist, then stepped back. The authorities would get the information from her eventually, but—

A flash of movement from one of the trucks near the tree line caught her attention. And features she recognized from photos sent her pulse racing. "Applewood," she muttered. "Steve! He's getting away!"

She slammed the door in Lila's face and took off after him, ignoring Steve's surprised shout, but taking notice of him closing in fast on her tail. Other officers gave chase as well, but Riley was closer. If not for the full moon in the sky, she would have lost him, but just enough light filtered through the branches for her to keep sight of the white shirt he wore.

Her feet pounded the ground and she drew closer, spurred on by adrenaline and rage, and tracked closely by Steve. There was no way he was going to get away.

Applewood tripped. His arms flailed as he fought to stay on his feet, but gravity won out. Riley didn't pause. She dove on top of the man and jammed her forearm against his throat. He gagged, coughed, and rolled, revealing a weapon in his right hand.

He started to turn it toward her when a foot kicked out and sent the gun spinning into the woods.

Riley rolled to the left and Steve grabbed the man by his arms and yanked them behind him.

Other officers arrived, weapons drawn and aimed at the three of them. "Nice tackle, ma'am," the nearest one said, lowering his weapon and holding out a hand. "I know a football team—or ten—that could use you."

Riley huffed a laugh and grasped the helping hand. He pulled her to her feet while one of the others pulled cuffs from his belt. "If you'll move, I'll take him off your hands."

"Can you get the sheriff?" Steve asked.

The man froze. "What?"

"The sheriff. I promised him he could cuff him. He's got a bullet in him and needs to get to a hospital but refused treatment until he could cuff Applewood. I'd like to give him that pleasure."

"I'm here," the sheriff's rough voice cut in.

Blood dripping from his reopened wound—thanks to his walk from the car to the wooded area—the man swayed.

One of the FBI team members gripped his arm and helped him over to Steve and the subdued prisoner, who was glaring but silent.

Saunders dropped to one knee, took the cuffs and placed them on Applewood's wrists. He looked up at Steve. "Thank you."

Then he promptly fell over unconscious.

Paramedics rushed over and Steve scrambled to his feet and out of the way. He went to Riley and pulled her into a hug. "You did it."

"No," she said, "we did it."

"Yeah. We did. Let's go home."

EPILOGUE

ne Week Later

THE KNOCK on Riley's door pulled her out of her Netflix stupor and into the foyer. She peered through the peephole to see Steve holding a bouquet of flowers. Her pulse thundered in her ears and she drew in a deep breath, fighting to control the hope that flared as she opened the door. "Hi."

"Hi." He handed her the flowers and she stepped back to let him in.

They'd gotten together everyday for the past week, but hadn't talked about what needed to be discussed. Today was the day. No more surface chatter. "Thanks, they're beautiful."

"I suppose it would be corny to say they're not as beautiful as you?"

"Corny . . . and a bit weird maybe." She shrugged. "But I'll take it."

He laughed and followed her into the kitchen, watching while she found a vase and settled the flowers into it. When she was finished—and looking for something else to help her stall so she wouldn't have to look at him—he came to her and placed his hands on her shoulders. She stilled and met his gaze. "I'm sorry," he said.

The out-of-the-blue apology left her speechless. She'd thought she was going to have to broach the subject they'd both been avoiding. It may seem weird to some to be together and not talk about the very thing that needed discussing the most, but they'd used the time to get to know one another again. To enjoy each other's company. Granted, some moments had been awkward with some heavy silences, but no more.

It was time...no more delays or procrastination. If they were going to have a future together, they had to clear up the past. She gave a slow nod. "Thank you."

"So . . . here it is. I didn't want to leave you, but my father . . ." He stopped and rubbed his eyes. "This is hard. Thank you for not pushing the issue." He paused. "Why haven't you?"

"Once I started to get over being angry, I could tell you needed some time."

"I'd planned to talk about it that day at lunch, but I think... I think I would have chickened out."

"And now?"

"I can't chicken out now. So, yes, my father. He's always been hardheaded, and he's always had his own plans for me."

"I know. You used to talk about being a doctor. Or an archaeologist."

"No, *you* talked about being an archaeologist."

"Oh. Right." She laughed. "Sorry."

"Anyway, I realized two years into the pre-med track, I didn't want to be a doctor."

"So, you joined the military."

"Yeah. I loved it, too."

She frowned. "Then why did you get out?"

"I realized I loved you more."

Tears welled and she sniffed. "So, you go off for four years. *Four years*, Steve. With barely a note or a call or a text." Okay, so maybe some of the anger was still there.

"I know, Riley. Please, believe me, I know. But I was—messed up when I left. And as time passed, I was so sure you'd moved on. I thought you'd have met someone else by now and that you might even have a kid or two. I was scared to death to find out," he said, his voice low, tinged with shame. "I've never considered myself a coward before, but I was when it came to you."

A tear slipped down her cheek, but her heart softened once more. "But why *leave*? I thought we had something special."

He blinked and looked away, a flush darkening his cheeks. "It's going to sound so stupid, I really don't even want to say it out loud."

"Say it. Please."

"What it boils down to is my father convinced me I wasn't good enough for you."

She gaped. "What?"

"He chose his tactics well. Instead of talking bad about you or trying to convince me *you* weren't good for *me*, he pointed out all of the amazing things you could do, how smart you were and"—he shrugged—"I don't know. It began to eat at me. He was right. You were definitely all of those things. You'd suffered a huge tragedy in the loss of your parents at a vulnerable age and come out a better person for it. You were way more mature than anyone else our age. You were flying planes before you could drive, for crying out loud. I was partying with the best of them and putting too much importance on Friday night football."

"That *was* important. At the time."

He shrugged. "At the time, but even then, my father was pushing me. Filling my head with lies that I believed. Telling me *his* plans for *my* life."

"And those plans didn't include me."

"No. They didn't. So, he worked on me, chipped away at my self-esteem until I started wondering if there was truth in his words. He's a psychiatrist, Riley, he knew what to say and how to say it. It wasn't until about two years ago that one of my unit buddies helped me understand what the man had done to me. Helped me push aside the lies to see through to the truth."

She fell silent, thinking. "I'm glad he was able to help you see that."

"Me, too."

More silence. She couldn't say the hurt wasn't still there, but the desire to move past it, not let it control her anymore was greater than the need to cling to past hurts. "When was the last time you talked to your father?"

He shook his head. "Last week when we got back from the compound."

"Really?"

"We have an understanding now. He doesn't try to run my life, and I don't tell my mom about his secret collection of motorcycles." He sighed. "He didn't even realize what he was doing—or if he did, he told himself he didn't. It was just his way of . . . getting what he wanted, I guess."

"But he didn't."

"No. And he apologized for interfering—for not supporting me."

She raised a brow. "What brought on the apology?"

"My mother threatened to leave him if he didn't. She was furious with him when I finally explained the reason for the tension between us."

"Wow. That's pretty intense."

He nodded. "But the damage had been done. It took a while to heal from that. The more I was away from him, the more I was able to filter through all of the negative stuff and get to the truth—of who I was and what I wanted."

"I'm sorry. Uncle Daniel has been nothing but supportive in everything I've ever wanted to do. My parents, too, before the car accident. Which was why I found the cult such a hard thing to understand. I can't fathom it."

"I can see how you would feel that way. But it's weird because I can see the draw of the cult as well—and how easy it might be to allow ones self to be sucked in to something you think is going to be the answer to your happiness. It's similar to what my father did to me when you think about it. I looked up to my dad, thought he was one of the smartest men I knew, so his words held weight." He shrugged. "I finally accepted his lies about me—and you—and made it my truth. Just like most of the Swiss Saints accepted everything Applewood fed them."

She could see that.

"But what about the sheriff and the others who had regular jobs and families and supported the cult financially anyway?"

He shook his head. "From what I understand, most of those people were planning to join at some point in the future. They could put a deposit down on their place, including noting how they would serve, what kind of dwelling place they would live in, and so on. And when they were ready, they'd be guaranteed entrance at a certain level of power."

She frowned. "So that's where the cardiologist came in."

"Exactly. He completely bought in to the whole end-of-the-world thing. Applewood had him convinced that his father would go through eternity with a bad heart if he didn't help—and his own eternal life would be affected if he didn't obey this call.

"A cardiologist. How can anyone so smart be so deceived?"

"It's not a matter of intelligence. When life—or another person—beats you down so hard and so low, sometimes an escape like that is extremely appealing. When people hurt, they look for ways to escape it. Mine was the Marines."

Riley nodded. "Mine was flying."

"Anyway, Applewood is still recovering from his surgery and will be heading back to prison to join the rest of his family—never to hurt or deceive anyone again. On this side of the prison anyway."

She sighed. "I'm so glad that's all over."

"Me too." He gripped her hands. Then pulled her into a hug. "Will you forgive me, Riley? And give me another chance?"

She nodded and looked up. "I've missed you so much. I knew you and your father weren't getting along, but I didn't know the root of it."

"I know. That's on me. Never again, okay? No secrets between us."

She smiled through the tears that kept springing up. "No secrets. Although I have to tell you one more."

He frowned. "What?"

"I think . . . I want to . . . um . . ."

"Come on, Riley, just spit it out."

"I think I want to join the FBI." The words came out in a rush and she bit her lip, waiting on his reaction.

He blinked. Then shrugged. "You'd make an amazing agent."

"Really?"

"Really."

"Just like that, you're okay with it?"

"Of course. It's your life and I'll support you in anything you want to do."

Riley's heart nearly burst. "You're the first person I've told."

"I'm honored." His lips settled over hers and she fell into the kiss. Warm, familiar, yet new. His presence wrapped around her, along with light and truth and the hope of a future with him. When he lifted his head, his eyes danced with expectation and a joy she'd never noticed before. "I love you, Riley," he said, his voice low and husky. "I think I've loved you forever. Out of all the truths that I've questioned, that one's never wavered."

"I love you too, Steve."

He hugged her again, holding her so tight, the breath left her. Then he laughed.

"What?" she asked, leaning back, but not wanting to let him go.

"Life. If I hadn't gone into the Marines, if I'd become a doctor, I never would have had the guts to go after you at the compound."

"Yes, you would have. You might not have had the skills, but you would have come."

He sighed and kissed the top of her head. "Yeah, I would have."

She pulled away but kept ahold of his hand to drag him to the couch. "Sit."

"Okay . . . Why?"

He dropped onto the sofa and she picked up the remote. "Because memory lane is calling."

She snuggled against him and clicked Play. Within seconds, the sound of the mockingjay—and Steve's laughter —filled the room.

Available Now

 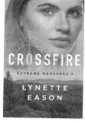 

Extreme Measures Series

Coming August 2023

www.lynetteeason.com

You asked for it and we listened!

Heroes in the Crossfire is now AVAILABLE in print!

Order yours now on Amazon.com
https://tinyurl.com/2874d7jb

Made in the USA
Middletown, DE
30 September 2023

39848906R00061